SHORELINE OF INFINITY

ISSUE 29: DECEMBER 2021

G000058159

**Award-winning science fiction magazine
published in Scotland for the Universe.**

ISBN: 978-1-8381268-8-9

ISSN 2059-2590

Submissions of fiction, art, reviews, poetry, non-fiction are
welcomed: visit the website to find out how to submit.

www.shorelineofinfinity.com

Publisher
Shoreline of Infinity Publications / The New Curiosity Shop
Edinburgh
Scotland

061221

Cover art: Stephen Daly

Contents

Editorial Team

Co-founder, Editor-in-Chief, Editor:
Noel Chidwick

Co-founder: Mark Toner

Deputy Editor & Poetry Editor: Russell Jones

Reviews Editor: Samantha Dolan

Non-fiction Editor: Pippa Goldschmidt

Art Director (Acting): Caroline Grebbell

Copy-editors: Pippa Goldschmidt, Russell Jones, Iain Maloney, Eris Young

Proof Reader: Cat Hellisen

Fiction Consultant: Eric Brown

First Contact

www.shorelineofinfinity.com

contact@shorelineofinfinity.com

Twitter: @shoreinf

. . . .

Thanks Sam!

This issue marks the last Shoreline *of Infinity with Sam Dolan as Reviews Editor. She took over the role for Issue 13 and has worked energetically with reviewers and publishers to build a strong reviews section in the magazine and on the website.*

We won't be losing her completely as she will continue to run the Quadrant Book Club. We wish Sam well and thank her for her stunning efforts and constant cheerfulness.

. . . .

Pull up a Log

Sit yourself down and I'll throw a log on the fire. Comfortable? Good. As the winter closes in about us let's share some ghost stories.

The task for our flash-fiction writers this year was to come up with a science fiction ghost story, and as ever, our reader-writers did not disappoint. The winning writers, **Ida Keogh, Ben Blow and Leigh Loveday**, each created a ghostly universe that sends a wee chill up your spine, but which is thoroughly science fictional.

What is a science fictional ghost? In non-genre space your ghost has to be the spirt of a dead person, but in SF, well, your imagination can take you anywhere you want to go. I particularly like that the winners each took a different route; bio-technological, alien planet and "techno-ghost Slavic Noir," to quote a judge. All top ten tales took on a different slant, and so did nearly all of the submitted entries. Some of the other stories might still see the light of day in Shoreline...

I'd like to say a big thank you to our judges. This was the third year where we invited University literature students to make up the judging panel, and again we were delighted by their skills and enthusiasm with which they took to the task. It's a pleasure every year to read the submissions through fresh eyes and insights that the students provide.

That's enough from me. Turn the page and Callum McSorley will take you on a journey to the hidden depths of the Antarctic ice in his story *The Great Nothing*.

Would you like another toasted martianmellow?

Noel Chidwick
Editor-in-Chief,
Shoreline of Infinity
December 2021

Great Nothing

Callum McSorley

R adio contact with Moscow crapped out while crossing the Indian Ocean. Interference was expected – Kazimir Station went dark weeks ago. Orlova was on her own, as she knew she would be.

She told the crew of the icebreaker she'd been sent to write a never-to-be-read report on the USSR's Antarctic research bases, but none of them believed it. They smelled KGB off her. She didn't care what they smelled. Once she was fit enough to walk

Art: Stephen Daly

again, she spent most of her time on deck, watching the aurora burn the sky. The drip-feed of out-of-date painkillers gave the colours a tangible quality. She could taste them.

By the time they hit land and dragged themselves into Mirny Station, it was daylight all the time, or what passed for daylight at night – a murky sickbed pall that drained the world.

Penguins on the shore watched the stevedores unload supplies, hooting at them in contempt from their hills of baked shit.

Orlova was expected, but not officially.

"I was wondering when someone would show up," Gurkovsky, the head researcher at Mirny, said. He was windburned and looked starving in a way particular to those who live in remote places. "We saw it from here, you know. The flash. Been trying to get a message out since… I even tried reaching my counterpart at Kazimir, Professor Usenko, but…" He shrugged and turned to the window of the cabin – a corrugated, insulated hut on runners that served as both admin and sleeping quarters. Outside, the spindrift swallowed the sailors in its waves.

The office door burst open and a man in full winter gear crashed in, tearing a balaclava from his red, wheezing face. "They're unpacking! They're bloody well unpacking out there!"

"Ivan…" Gurkovsky put up his hands, as if approaching a small but potentially vicious animal. "I told you they wouldn't be evacuating. There's—"

"No need? No bloody need? I want off this frozen rock, I—"

"You can go back with the ship if you want," Orlova said.

The scientist called Ivan noticed Orlova then, noticed what the sailors had noticed before – the way she carried herself, the careful neutrality of her expression, the steel eyes, the bulge under the right arm that hinted at another kind of steel. "You … you can authorise that?"

"No," she said. "But you can go if you want, nobody will stop you."

He pointed his balaclava at her. "This whole thing stinks. They don't give a shit, do they? They don't…" The hat fell to his side. He turned away, turned back, turned away again and headed out the door.

"Ivan!" Gurkovsky called. "Door!" But he didn't come back.

Orlova closed it herself. Gurkovsky noticed the wince, her hand twitching to her belly, as she moved too fast towards the door. "Who was the ship doctor?" he said.

"Bukin."

"Well, it could've been worse. Dmitriyev did mine, the old drunk, was lucky he didn't take a kidney by mistake. Could've died over an operation I didn't even need. Still, better than what happened to Rogozov."

Dr Leonid Rogozov had been Novolazarevskaya Station's sole physician a few years back; he got appendicitis out there and had to remove the organ by himself before it burst. Since then, anyone heading into the Antarctic interior was offered an elective appendicectomy. Orlova wasn't going to bother until Bukin showed her the footage on the projector in the ship's rec room. "Took him long enough but the bastard did it," Bukin had said, smiling.

"When are you heading out to Kazimir?" Gurkovsky asked.

"As soon as the tractor is ready."

"I'll start heating it up."

The lamps of the tractor-train punched twin holes through the forever-twilight of the Antarctic summer. Orlova hauled herself up over the treads of the second trailer and pulled herself through the carriage door. She was about to shut out the sub-zero cold when a figure, hunched against the wind, came waddling over from the admin hut, waving its arms. It moved without grace but in a way totally adapted to the world it inhabited – the unreliable ground, the wind blast.

Gurkovsky pulled the scarf down off his face and lifted his visor. Snow began to settle on his brows and eyelashes. He was out of breath when he shouted up: "I've got to ask, not so much for myself but for the others. Are we going to be left to die out here?"

"This is the only place colder and more remote than Siberia," Orlova said – *except the moon, and if they could send us there they would have.* "You were dead when you arrived."

Day and night passed without much difference. The radio stayed silent, Orlova stayed in her makeshift quarters in the second carriage. Out the window, the foam spray of diamond dust fizzed in the wind, blown from peaks of snow. They detoured around canyons made of cracked ice and scaled frozen dunes, heading into the heart of the great nothing: Kazimir, the coldest place on Earth.

The train stopped. It often did, for various reasons, each of which Orlova left the driver, Mikhail, and his crew to deal with. She trusted the rough old man's expertise, his years of hard-won experience on the hostile continent. He was a useful man, but smug about it. He came banging at the door.

"Secret agent! Secret agent!" he called.

"Shut up, you old bear," Orlova replied. "What do you want?"

He stepped aside so Orlova had a clear view out the carriage door and swept his hand across the barren vista.

"What am I looking at?" Orlova said, but she was already starting to understand. There were odd white humps piled in a rough circle – rough but not rough enough. *Arranged.* They weren't snow banks.

She grabbed her gear together and jumped down onto the snow while still pulling her balaclava on, her gloves held in one hand – the fingers instantly numb in the painful air. It hurt to breathe. She used her teeth to get the gloves on and stomped over to the nearest hump. She gave it a kick with her boot and it made a dull thud. "Rooftops..."

"They've not been digging it out, I guess," Mikhail said. "Still here though. That's something, eh?"

"Yes, yes it is…" So Kazimir Station wasn't a smoking crater after all, but it was now underneath them, buried up to the hairline in packed snow. "Get the lamps out, and the shovels," she ordered.

"But it's the middle of the night," Mikhail said, with a hint of a smile at the sickly pall of daylight around them. "The men—"

"—I've got a bottle of vodka and five cartons of cigarettes for each of them in my carriage."

"You know the saying 'when hell freezes over'?"

"It already has. Get to work."

Orlova joined the dig. It was warmer working outside than staying still in the carriage – the paraffin heaters were being used to stop the tractor's engine from freezing while it was switched off. Although the cold burned inside her lungs, she felt sweat trickling down her back. Her gun chafed at her ribs under the layers of deep-winter clothing. The pain in her abdomen twinged every time she drove the blade of the shovel into the snow. She was about to call a break when a shout went up.

They'd been digging around the nearest dome, trying to work their way down until they found a door. They hadn't found it yet. They found something else first.

"Well-preserved, except for a bit of freezer burn," Mikhail said, looking down at the stiff, blue body of a man not dressed for the cold. His unprotected face was a crystal mask of twisted horror, his eyes wide open, his jaw hanging down to almost touch his chest. Frostbite had taken his nose and fingers, and the patches of exposed skin that weren't blue were black with rot. Orlova patted him down and came away with only a crumpled pack of cigarettes – *Laikas*, Russian – and their lighter. There was something on his wrist – immediately Orlova's mind went to handcuffs or some other kind of restraint but looking closer she saw it was a bracelet. Hanging on the chain like a lucky charm was a swastika carved from steel and painted black.

11

She snapped it from its chain and held it up to the half-dead sun, taking off her glove and turning it over and round and feeling its edges with numb fingertips.

"Nazis in Kazimir," Mikhail said, and whistled, the note steaming out in a cloud from his lips.

Orlova stuck the trinket in her jacket pocket. "We'll see."

Another metal swastika had been made into a pendant, found hanging around the throat of second frozen man. His face was in equal ruin to the first one, also in a rigid scream. They laid them side by side a good distance from the tractor-train and covered them with a tarp weighed down at its corners by snow.

The cause of death wasn't freezing for the third one that turned up.

"Now, if I was a man who knew his Antarctic exploration, I'd say that was done with a climbing axe," Mikhail said, pointing to the deep puncture in the top of the dead man's skull.

They'd found him curled up, his face protected by his arm. No swastika amulet on the wrist. Orlova pried the arm out of the way. "I know this man," she said. "Tatarovich."

"KGB?"

"Yeah. CIA too."

Mikhail chuckled. "You people do have your fun."

"Well, you're the one living out in Antarctica, old bear. I guess you had your fun too."

Mikhail wrestled open a bottle of vodka with his gloves still on and raised it in a toast. "To fun!"

They worked in shifts and slept in the tractor-train. They set up a series of posts strung together with rope between the train and the dig site, in case the weather got bad. It was only a short distance but if a whiteout hit, visibility would be zero and being stuck outside would mean joining the stiffs under the tarp.

By the time they'd dug down to the door, they'd uncovered another two bodies – a man and a woman. One with a swastika, one without. One frozen stiff and screaming, the other stabbed with a piton, the steel spike still buried in their chest. "That's a lung-shot," Orlova said. "She drowned."

"So what happened, then? Half of them turned out to be Nazis, half American spies, and they punched it out?" Mikhail was doing more drinking than digging now. "What about the radio interference, the flash, you know? What happened to the bomb?"

Orlova shrugged. "Not for you to worry about."

They finished clearing the door.

The vault door creaked open. A hiss of warm, stale air turned to steam as it rushed out to meet the crew, shrouding them in a mist of bad breath.

Orlova stepped in first. Snow was still packed up over most of the windows, so the chamber was dark. Her torch swept over benches and boots, and racks of jackets and hats and visors. A shadow board held crampons, ice shoes, ropes, and assorted climbing gear. The stink of wet furs lay heavy in the stuffy air.

In the centre of the hut were two snow mobiles loosely covered by tarpaulins. The heaters surrounding the machines were switched off. "Both broken," Mikhail said. The rustle of plastic sheets as he poked around the scooters with his torch was obnoxiously loud in that dark, quiet place. "Deliberate too. They've been tampered with. Not by a mechanic but by someone who knew enough to do the damage."

Chatter broke out among the crew.

"Quiet," Orlova commanded. The men shut up. The silence was dense. Orlova felt the snow pressing in from above as she moved through the door into an adjoining corridor.

The next domed room, behind the hermetic hiss of another door, was fitted out with lab benches and assorted equipment. Orlova's torch swept across a wall hung with charts and graphs. Dominating them was a large, detailed sketch of a drill boring down into the ice of off-white paper. It dug down two-and-a-half miles before it hit a hatched bowl labelled "Lake Kazimir".

"What were they up to?" Mikhail asked, creeping up behind her.

"Officially, drilling out ice cores, seeing what's inside."

"Unofficially?" Mikhail turned away from the wall and scanned the high-tech tomb around him.

"I thought you'd guessed already."

"I thought I had, but there's nothing here that looks like nuc – Shit!" Mikhail dropped his torch and slammed backwards against a table, sending paperwork to the floor. "What the fuck is *that?*"

Orlova spun around while Mikhail scrambled on the floor, flailing for his torch. On a shelf on the opposite wall was a large specimen jar. Inside the briny fluid was something tentacular and strange. It was dead, bloated and pushing up against the lid of the jar. The tuberous body was covered in fine hair, its appendages looking both strong and soft.

"Some kind of squid," Orlova said.

"A squid?" Mikhail was panting. "Look at its fucking eyes! A squid…"

Orlova counted three of them that she could see from this side of the jar. Each one frozen open, though half-covered by the sagging hood of an eyelid – staring, myopic, clouded with death.

The others tramped in and the panic started.

"What the—"

"Holy—"

"Mother—"

"We need to get out!"

"Run!"

The shot dropped them all to their knees; the flash scorched their retinas. They looked round, blinking and rubbing at their ringing ears, to see Orlova still standing, gun in the air, the heat of the powder explosion bathing her in a curling cloud of steam and grey gun-smoke.

Orlova was glad the luger still functioned at all in this temperature. "Go back to the train and wait inside," she said, as if talking to schoolboys. "Not you," she added, as Mikhail turned to go with them. "You might be useful, old bear."

Together they pushed on into the next chamber. Mikhail chattered as they went. "Maybe it was the tests, you know, the radioactivity? It gets into the wildlife and—"

"You said yourself there's no evidence of tests like that being carried out here."

"But we've not seen the whole place yet…"

They tiptoed through silent sleeping quarters. The bunks were crammed in tight. Photographs and knick-knacks littered the area, the detritus and decoration of those far from home. Chess boards and playing cards spoke of meandering, half-finished games, meagre respite from the crushing loneliness and boredom of the off-shift hours.

A plastic tub on a side-table contained a collection of little black, metal swastikas.

The drill room was vast compared to the other huts; its roof vaulted with ribs of rivetted steel. Plastic, wipe-clean floor tiles around the circumference gave way to smooth ice. In the centre, the mean-toothed helix of the drill bit hung suspended from a rusted red tower weighted at each of its four feet by huge spools of cable. The ice hole was a little wider than a person's shoulders in diameter and perfectly circular. By its smooth edge was a harness and a winch.

"They've been down then," Orlova said, inspecting the belts and buckles.

"To where?" Mikhail was kneeling as close to the edge of the hole as he dared, shining his torch down. Blackness.

"Lake Kazimir."

"A lake below the ice?"

Orlova nodded. "Want to see it?" She held out the harness.

"Go down there?" He barked a sarcastic laugh. "No thanks, besides, the hole looks too narrow for me, my shoulders..." He trailed off as Orlova started laughing.

"Your beer gut, more like. I need you to work the winch," she said, already climbing into the straps.

"Up here by myself?" He felt his pocket for his bottle.

"Here's some company." She handed over her gun. "Might have to take your gloves off to use it with those big paws of yours, old bear."

He was about to protest but then didn't. "Make sure the leg straps are tight around your thighs," he said, "if they're loose and you fall, when the safety catches, they'll ride up and rip your balls off."

The light at the top of the tunnel became a pinprick then disappeared altogether. Orlova switched on her helmet torch. It reflected off the ice wall in front of her face. The tunnel was narrow, she could hear the toes of the crampons Mikhail had given her – along with his ice axe – dragging against the ice as she descended. The *scritch-scritch* it made was the only sound other than her ragged breathing, now she could no longer hear the motor of the winch. Blood pulsed in her ears.

Two-and-half-miles. Straight down. Vertical drop. Don't think about it. The harness cut into her, it was tight enough. Breathe. Close your eyes. Count to ten. Do it again. Long way to go. Two-and-half, two-and-a-half...

Shining the torch down she could see little more than a black gap between her knees and the flash of the spiked crampons on her boots. The ground came as a shock and she found herself sitting on a smooth, frozen surface, the intense cold burning through her clothes and backside and up her spine.

She tugged hard on the cable to signal Mikhail but it continued to unwind, falling into a loose snake-coil on the packed ice until it stopped with a shudder.

Along with the light on her helmet, Orlova had her torch and a few flares which she'd found among boxes of dynamite and other blasting equipment at the drill site. She snapped one on and in the brilliant red light she found herself standing on the frozen beach of Lake Kazimir. The ice slid downwards and gave way to a rocky shoreline. The crags and boulders flashed with red from the flare and bounced her torchlight up to the stalactites that hung way above, dripping. The lake beyond was mirror-glazed and smoking. A rotten-egg fog roiled over its surface.

Orlova launched the flare as high and far as she could.

She traced its progress, its light no longer touching the stalactites which had shrunk back, higher and higher, into darkness. As it came down a red circle grew across the lake's surface – she could see no opposite bank – then it fizzed as it splashed down and was lost. The diagram in the lab had estimated the lake to be some miles long and wide. It hadn't guessed at a depth.

She snapped another flare and dug its handle into the ice by the cable, then she unclipped the harness. She began to skirt the bank by torchlight, the warm hiss of the flare getting further away. She moved closer to the rocks and the slope where the glassy water met the shore, hidden by its folds of mist.

Something moved. In the water. Orlova held her breath, counted to ten. She scanned the surface with the torch. There it was! The surface broke and waves lapped out towards her. She saw a smooth hide and then something made a splash – a fin, a flipper? Something alive in there. She thought of the dead thing stuffed into the specimen jar, the sagging skin around eyes that looked almost human.

A skittering noise behind her: on the icy rock wall, many legs disappeared from the glare of her searchlight.

Then the hiss and huff of a water jet behind. As she spun to face the water, Orlova slipped and, in a flurry of shredded ice, she landed on the ground, knocking the wind from her belly and the torch from her hand. Her head, protected by the helmet, cracked off a rock, making a loud thud that rang inside her skull and put out the headlamp.

The dark was absolute.

Then it wasn't.

The subterranean world was ablaze in blues and greens and purples, light so ethereal and vivid it was as if the ground had opened up above and Orlova was once again staring, dazzled and drugged, at the Aurora Australis. The walls and ceiling of the catacombs were crawling with pulsing light. Shadows flapped and flew across the deep shadows in the crevices of stalactites. There were legs and feelers and so many eyes.

Standing, Orlova looked out across the shining lake, now alive with sparkling ripples, and monstrous bodies curling through the water in corkscrews. She could see now the true scale of Lake Kazimir, its startling beauty, its secret.

Something breached the water – the top of a head and eyes – moving towards her. She pressed herself back against a boulder, her hand went instinctively to the holster on her side. Empty. It hauled itself up onto the rocks and ice, its snout a good two feet ahead of the rest of it. Its limbs, both clawed and webbed, were striped with green-blue bioluminescence, as was its back and tail. Slick fur covered the space in between. It snuffled its way up to Orlova, still too weak-kneed to run. The twitch of its nose was like a grasping hand opening and closing. It squeezed its way, sniffing, over her boots and legs, then turned and carried on its way up the bank.

Orlova walked back to the red signal flare, now just a blip of fake colour among the organic glow of the beasts and the lapping waves of the lake. She strolled, watching the water and the recesses in the cave walls where the ice glittered like diamond. Ancient birds and insects approached her with curiosity then left her to go on her way – no reason to feel threatened by her presence. It was a dream. She hooked herself back onto the cable and gave it a languid tug to signal Mikhail. Some wonderful dream…

She tugged again, and again got no response. And again.

Now she was wide awake, as if she'd been plunged into cold water, adrenaline panic-pumping through her organs and arteries. "Mikhail!?" Her voice echoed around the vast underground chamber. She screamed up from the bottom of the well and got nothing but her own terror bouncing back.

Breathe. Count to ten. She paced and swore. Calm down. Think. Panic nearly made her throw up. Trapped. "At least there's plenty of food down here," she said, and rattled off a manic giggle. Think, breathe, count.

"Right... right..." She wrapped the cable around one arm and took a good grip with both hands. She planted a spiked boot against the ice wall of the tunnel, kicking hard to dig the crampons in for a firm foothold. Then she began to climb. The tunnel was narrow enough she could brace her back against it and walk her feet up the other side without stretching her legs too far. Slowly, slowly, she began to squeeze herself upwards into the dark. Two-and-half-miles. Don't think about it. Breathe.

She would dig in her ice axe every so often to give her hands a break from the cable. Her stops became more and more frequent. The pain in her belly was sickening, she put her hand to it and squeezed as if trying to hold her insides together. The blue-green blaze of the tunnel below had gone and for a long time she climbed on in total darkness. She swore to herself, and to Mikhail, that coward, that traitorous bastard! Two-and-a-half...

When her body was burning and sore and ready to give up, she saw it: a single star up above. She shuffled and heaved and climbed till the star got bigger and closer and opened its mouth. A great scream rose up from her belly and all the strength left in her body was spent heaving herself over the edge of the tunnel and back into the drill room. She lay there for a time with her eyes closed, sucking in air, the deep cold making her shiver, exhaustion making her tremble.

Finally tipping herself upright, she noticed another figure in furs slumped on the ground over by the handle of the winch. It was Mikhail. His head and face had been punctured, over and over, now a jellied mass of blue-veined meat. A spike, or a climbing axe... The gun was gone, his index finger chewed off at the knuckle.

Orlova took his torch and began to move towards the lab, through the sleeping quarters and the boot room with the sabotaged snow mobiles. She kept herself low and close to the walls. Every so often she stopped in a crouch and covered the beam of the torch with her hand, held her breath, listening. Nothing.

The front door they'd come through was open, the snow already starting to spill inside. It was starting to come down heavy. Thick flakes fell in a dizzy pattern. Orlova grabbed the guide rope they'd set up and worked her way, hand over hand, towards the tractor-train, blinking snow from her eyes. She couldn't see the light of the lamps heating the tractor's engine.

She hauled herself up into the first carriage and could already smell stale cordite, spent gunpowder, the rank sewer-stench of a gut-shot. One of them – what was his name? Egor? – was on the floor of the first carriage, marinating in his own blood, intestines leaking from the holes in his belly. The rest were in the second carriage, laid out here and there like reclining figures in a Renaissance painting, blood spray on the walls and ceiling.

Orlova felt for the axe that should have been on her belt. It wasn't there, she'd left it dug into the mouth of the tunnel.

She took tentative steps through the mess, stepping over splayed limbs. Something grabbed her ankle – her mind jumped to the snuffling nose of the animal that had crawled out of the lake below and she jumped, pulling away. One of them was still alive. He flailed and made gurgling noises – Orlova could see the hole where the bullet had gone through the man's throat. He waved and gesticulated in a manic spasm, his eyes wide, screaming. He made desperate, rasping grunts. Too late, Orlova understood what he was trying to say.

The blow would have killed her if it wasn't for her helmet. Instead, the axe plunged into the hard plastic and only the tip pierced the top of her head. She turned, tangled; a painful tug ripped the helmet off, the straps grazing her chin and ears. Orlova lashed out with a kick, felt it connect, and a blind punch sent shockwaves up her elbow on impact. She righted herself and faced the barrel of a gun. A figure wrapped in furs, hidden by scarves and goggles held it, shaking.

Orlova's hand flashed out for the attacker's wrist; the gun went off. The bullet sliced the side of Orlova's head, taking a chunk of her ear with it. She hit the deck, ear ringing, warm blood running down her cheek and jaw. She tasted it on her lips.

Something heavy came down on top of her skull and put the lights out.

Orlova sat up for a moment then lay back down again. She wasn't ready. Her head... her ear... everything throbbed and hurt, made her feel queasy. A crust of dry blood covered her face and matted her hair.

From the ground she could see the red frame of the tower and the dangling drill bit. With her face against the ice she could see the hump of Mikhail's body. It started to move, sliding along, being hauled by a furred creature with reflective, goggled eyes. It dragged him by the handle of an axe, the angular blade buried deep under his jaw like a fish hook in a gill.

The eyes fixed on Orlova. It pulled the scarf down from its mouth and nose. "You're awake already." A woman's voice. She smiled.

Orlova forced herself up into a sitting position.

The goggles came off, revealing a pleasant, middle-aged face with a flaking tan and deepening cracks around the eyes. "You've impressed me, you know. Climbing up the tunnel? Good god!" She shook off a glove and pulled Orlova's gun from inside her coat. "Did you like it down there?" She was smiling, nervous, like she really cared what Orlova would say about it.

"It's something all right," Orlova said, her voice a dry croak.

The woman grinned. "Uh huh. Something. Something special, right?"

Orlova nodded then regretted moving her head. "You're Usenko, right?"

21

"Uh huh. Professor Vera Usenko, head researcher." Her smile was still nervous, but eager too. "And you are an agent, I'm guessing?"

"KGB. Orlova."

"Impressive. We had one of your spies in here, you know. A double-agent I believe."

"Tatarovich. I knew him."

"How nice. Were you friends?"

"No, he was a prick."

Usenko laughed at that.

Orlova shuffled, trying to get into a position where she could more easily get to her feet – lucky she still had the spikes on her boots, she was sitting on an ice rink. Usenko put the gun on her. "Stay still," she said. Orlova clocked the swastika hanging from a wool bracelet on her wrist.

"Even so, I'd like to know why you killed him… and everyone else."

"You went down there in the dark, didn't you? What did you see?"

"Light."

"Uh huh… Beautiful light. Powerful light."

"Powerful…"

"Energy. A source of energy, an incredible source, like nothing else we've ever seen. It's ancient, it's organic, it's… sacred. Did you feel it?"

"I saw the animals, they were glowing." Orlova doubted the memory now, it was like a dream.

"They create it, produce it. Pure, clean energy. You could light a city with it or launch a rocket."

"Or blow shit up."

Usenko seemed to communicate entirely in smiles – this one was pained. "Uh huh," she said.

"And you're, what? Selling it to some far-right group?"

"Wha—oh!" Usenko held up her arm to show the pendant clearly. "You mean this." She chuckled. "No, no, we just found a bunch of these when we were digging. During the war, the Germans dropped bucket-loads of these things all over the continent, trying to lay claim to it, I guess. Just a little keepsake. A small piece of history."

"So why did you kill the others then?"

"I can't let anybody find out about this. Not Washington, and not Moscow. You know what they'd do to this place if they knew... You know what it's like already, you're in the KGB for god's sake!" She was looking somewhere far away now, beyond the sights of the gun, beyond Orlova. "I poisoned most of them at dinner. The ones I missed I had to give a more personal touch to. It took days to drag them all out, but the snow covered them quick enough."

"You want to 'save the aliens'."

"It's not alien life, it's ancient life. Native. Older than us, older than the dinosaurs... which brings us to the point. What do *you* know about them?" The barrel of the gun came to bear again.

"Only what you've told me, and what I've seen for myself." Orlova caught the drift here. "They think this place went down in a nuclear accident. You set that up, right?"

"Uh huh... I... *harvested* some of their power..."

"Well, it worked. They don't know anything. You let me live, I go back and tell them Kazimir is a smoking dent in the Earth, case closed."

"And why are your crew all dead?"

"Whiteout, lost in the snow. Tragic." Orlova was slowly getting up now, keeping her hands up, visible, in front of her. "And what about you? Are you going to just starve out here under the snow?"

"I've got rations to last me a while, now there's nobody else to feed." A giggle. "Once I was sure this place was deep enough and nobody else would find it, I would... When the time is right, I'll just... head down there." She looked to the black mouth of the tunnel that dropped straight down into Lake Kazimir. "I thought I'd maybe like to go for a swim."

"It could be put to good use, you know. Clean energy…"

"It wouldn't though. You know it wouldn't." Finally, all the smiles were gone. Usenko approached, gun raised. "Besides, no matter the use, harvesting it all would destroy this place. And they would want it all. They can't help themselves. Neither can you. It's too late." Usenko pulled the trigger.

The gun gave a dry click that echoed off the hard ice and the metal dome above their heads. One short of a full magazine – Orlova had put the first bullet into the ceiling of the laboratory.

Usenko's eyes widened. She dropped the gun and went for the axe in her belt. Orlova drew her out, let her make her move, her mistake… She waited for the swing and caught her wrist as it came arcing down. With her left foot dug into the glass surface of the ice by the spikes on her boot, she lifted her right and kicked out, hoofing Usenko in the belly, sending her backwards. Usenko lost the axe as she went down and hit the ice with a hard crack. The momentum sent her sliding towards the mouth of the hole. She scrambled with bare fingers but the ice was slick and smooth. Her hand caught the handle of the axe Orlova had left dug into the edge of the hole. Usenko hung there for a moment, legs dangling over the two-and-a-half mile drop straight down to Lake Kazimir. "Don't," she wheezed, "don't let them—" The axe came loose.

Orlova heard Usenko scream for a time as she went down the tunnel, but the noise was lost well before she hit the bottom.

Orlova gathered up the axe and the empty gun and left the drill room for the comparative warmth of the sleeping quarters – she'd do something about Mikhail's body later, after she caught her breath and patched herself up. She washed her face in the sink of the communal latrine, inspecting the bite the bullet had taken out the top half of her ear, the edges of the wound singed and clotted. She couldn't get a look at the damage done to the top of her head but she could feel a swollen egg there and the tender edges of a gash running through the middle of it – Christ, what had she been hit with?

As Usenko had said, there was plenty of food and water in the station – and more out in the train carriages – and Orlova helped herself.

When she was ready, she pulled open the front door. "Shit. Whiteout." The snow was driving down in an intense flurry so thick the world outside had disappeared. She couldn't even see the first guidepost, let alone the train… The train! The snow would be well up over its caterpillar tracks by the time the storm was over, and with the lamps not heating the engine it was safe to say Orlova wasn't leaving the way she arrived.

Well, someone else would come along looking eventually. Maybe. She thought about what she'd said to Gurkovsky before leaving Mirny: "You were dead when you arrived." But what if they did come? She thought of the lake and its secrets, its wondrous beauty, that ancient dreamworld. Usenko was right, they would take it and exploit it, for good or bad.

There was dynamite in the drill room, she thought, peering out at the snow-blind world.

Callum McSorley is an author based in Glasgow. His short stories have appeared in New Writing Scotland, Monstrous Regiment, Gutter, and Shoreline of Infinity among others and in 2019 he was shortlisted for The Big Issue Crime Writing Competition.
You can find him on Twitter @CallumMcSorley
and at callummcsorley.com.

Relay

Louise Hughes

R elay 41 to Paige: *Are you awake yet?*

I woke up light-headed and light-bodied, drifting in my cabin with the carpet tiles and the rest of the station above my head. No one else breathed within a billion kilometres. Noa had been gone for twenty-three days.

Me: *I'm awake.*

I tapped the words into the air above my left wrist. Then I dialled up the gravity a bit and re-discovered the floor. I'd been running a challenge last night with Sadie (Relay 48). Repairs in low-g in the event of system failure. The lights were still set to evening, a dull candle glow instead of the bright white of morning. I must have overridden them.

Me to Relay 164: *Good morning. Remember to hydrate.*

I reached for my flask as I sent the message.

Relay 164: *Good morning.*

Art: Elen I I

We weren't close. I rarely saw them on the feed but they were my assigned morning contact today, just like I was Relay 41's. Sole working regulations stipulate regular check-ins with another human, except during sleep hours, and around half of the Deep Space Relay and Distribution Stations in the network are solo staffed. The rest have two operators. It takes a particular kind of person to want to live and work so far out from anywhere.

I completed my checks before breakfast. I like to eat without the paperwork hanging over me. Everything was tight, everything was working correctly, and I had the day's list. It was just another day in the floating warehouse that I called home.

Kevan (Relay 41): *Asa, did you find those seeds?*

Asa (Relay 43): *Yes, the bot misfiled them. They're ready for pickup.*

Kevan: *I can't believe they got their hothouses up and running so quickly. I thought they'd be on food crates for a few months yet.*

Asa: *Jealous? You know I only deal with the best and brightest.*

Me: *Settler groups are randomly assigned*

Asa: *That's what you think.*

Kevan had had three new settler groups through Relay 41 this month – two to join other groups on already settled worlds in his jurisdiction and one to a new moon.

Porridge bowl in hand, I started down the loading hall that ran almost the full circumference of the station's lowest, storage level. I'd made a cup of tea first thing but damned if I knew where I'd put it, and it wasn't 0900 yet. We run on twenty-four-hour days, all across the Relay Sphere. It ensures continuity for the freight pilots, and the paperwork. We all like continuity out here in the deep.

"Sap?"

"Working."

"Whereabouts?"

"Store B."

I took my porridge to the store and sat outside the door, watching the stars through the wide hall window. Sap came drifting out just as I remembered where I'd left my tea – by the transmitter station in the second level, when I was sending the check-in signals to the settlements. I'd had to wait. The Cascade Group – ten families, they'd been out here four years now – had been late with their return signal. They'd turned the job over to Tom Cascade, the newly minted teen. Something about responsibility.

Sap hovered in front of the window, status light blinking in that considering way. "I finished preparing the stock for Yen Group. We can send a request today, if you want."

I like to be a week ahead with stock, as the big freight ships move so slowly. I also have my doubts about the efficiency of the Earth system warehouses, based on the packing of the freight ships' holds. Noa assured me it was done by algorithm every time I complained.

My settler groups know to have their orders in early.

"We haven't had any new settler groups at all this month."

"Checking."

Sap's access to the band was faster than mine. I had to deal with the UI but they went direct. Machines deal quickly with machines. I'm only really here in case anything breaks, and because the Settler Council back home knows the settlers like a human proxy. When they show up, they talk to me and not to Sap. They talk about books and shows and feeds and art, all of which Sap likes as well. They talk endlessly, like they've just shown up from a silent religious order.

They say it's lonely out here in the dark.

"There are three pending groups. Two Council sponsored. One self-funded. Assignment deadline in ten days."

"I suppose. What if they're waiting for Noa's replacement to get here first?"

Sap didn't answer that. They're efficient, like I like to be, but better at it. They don't waste power on telling me the same thing twice. No one was replacing Noa unless my psych approves it. Noa might never be replaced.

"Marin Group have their assessment and check-ups in four days."

"The calendar's clear?"

"I contacted Relay 41 and 43 to ensure re-routing of transmission traffic."

I wouldn't be able to get onto the feeds until the evaluations were done. All our bandwidth would be needed to relay their calls to the Settler Council psych office. I tapped a reminder into the system, so I had enough reading material. It would affect the downloads as well.

"I'll request system checks on the buoys between here and Earth."

If everything was working properly, they'd be finished faster and I could reclaim my system. As long as there weren't any issues that Marin Group had forgotten to advance file. Some settler groups like to leave everything until the quarterly and it's not as efficient a way of doing things as they think. It clogs up my system and means I can't do things when I normally do them.

Sap stays out of my way on evaluation days. Sometimes I throw things.

"Incoming." The alert system pinged us both. I'd switched off all the annoying flashing lights and sirens.

Neither of us moved. We weren't expecting anyone. I checked the schedule again, because I hadn't finished my cup of tea and that can lead to mistakes. No. Our freight delivery wasn't due for two days and the last one had gone far enough past our area that it would be closer to an outlying border-post than us. I don't really talk to border posts. They're on orbiting planets and continually moving. The ones assigned to my route change all the time.

Me: *Unexpected incoming.*

I pinged the feed and received a series of one word and gesture icon responses back.

Asa: *Have you run a scan?*

Me: *Will do.*

Normally, I wouldn't have bothered them with it. We do get people showing up randomly. Settlers who forget to ping ahead, because they don't understand why it's important. I need to be ready, and how hard is it really to send a quick update? Then I can have the required repair bots and parts ready for their arrival. But no, they treat everything like they're living on a wild frontier.

Anyway, I was on monitoring. Because of Noa. Everywhere was quieter than it should be.

I moved to the nearest access station and ran the scans. The system confirmed the approach of a Type-C vessel – the kind used to ferry supplies, but generally not large numbers of people. They hadn't filed an incoming request so I got the system to ping them a reminder. It's not uncommon, like I said.

Sap ran a calculation while I was doing that.

"They're coming in from the starboard side, sixty-five degrees vertical."

There were four settler groups in that direction, assuming they'd flown straight and not stopped off anywhere. I pulled up a chart for confirmation.

Asa: *Is everything okay?*

Me: *They still haven't filed a request.*

Kevan: *Their transmitter might be damaged.*

Switch to manual. The system checked for a Morse signal first, while transmitting a repeated pattern on the two outboard lights. We also sent a request to the ship's system to allow us to access their internal telemetry, to see what we were dealing with as far as repairs went.

Nothing.

Me: *They're not even transmitting light signals.*

I needed to be in the centre. The access terminals in the landing hall are fine, but they don't have the same resources. Their UI is terrible.

Me: *Are you busy there?*

Asa: *I'm expecting freight this afternoon.*

Kevan: *Just paperwork for me.*

Me: *Can you boost me?*

Kevan: *I'll do it.*

A brief outline of the situation began its journey around the Relay Sphere. It's quicker to send a signal one-by-one than attempt to transmit to everyone at the same time, particularly those on the opposite side of the central Earth system.

By the time I got the ping back around from Asa on the other side, I was in the centre. The consoles there were familiar. I moved across them faster. Especially since Sap had moved Noa's chair out of the way and into Overflow Storage.

"Sap, can you stay by the docking port?"

I'd left them locking down the stores, as we did whenever anyone approached. Standard procedure. It's on the rules pinned to the centre wall. Some people choose to greet docking ships personally but I don't unless there's a problem. Sometimes, I stay up here in the centre the entire time they're here.

Everything is automated. But the system flashed up an error.

No request received.

Whether because of damage or laziness, they hadn't transmitted their docking code. Without it, the system wouldn't let them dock.

Don't imagine this is unusual behaviour. People forget all the time. Other people. People not me. The way I work, I run through the same process every time in the same order, so I can't forget. They approach life haphazardly. Noa used to be a bit like that. Things had become a lot more efficient on my Relay in the last three weeks.

I tried another reminding ping and got nowhere.

I've found that a lot of people swipe away reminders automatically. You can remind them four, five times, and they'll deny ever receiving it.

By then, I had the cameras on my screens. I'm the only one with access to them, and they're one of the reasons I'm here. I can study an image and work out things Sap can't, and the system can't. I can decide, based on what I see, whether to override automation.

I overrode it. The ship was from Marin Group, according to the markings, so they were coming up on their eval. Marin

Group had checked in as usual that morning but there had been no messages to tell me about the ship. Marin Group were medium efficiency settlers, with too much spontaneity for my liking. They did things like decide to throw a pasta festival and then complain I didn't have the flour supplies already.

I would be staying up here in the centre until they went away.

As the ship slowed towards the docking port, a cable snaked out to greet them. I had instructed the system to prioritise it so we could communicate over a hard connection before I opened the gate. I do not let anyone through the gate until we've debriefed. They tend to wander about. They try to help with things that are automated and complain when I remind them, because they're "just trying to help".

The line between help and getting in the way is very, very, thin.

Asa: *Status?*

Me: *Attempting to communicate via a hard connection. The ship is from Marin Group.*

The information was added to the boost cycle.

"Relay Station to Marin C Ship, over."

"This is Marin Ship. We're having trouble with our transmitter, over"

"Please send repair request and manifest, over."

"Acknowledged. Relay out."

There was something off with the manifest. It had all the information but in slightly the wrong order. The repair details were also sketchy and I re-read them a couple of times.

"Marin Ship here. Can you open the gate?"

Over. Impatience. You'd think people who'd travelled three days to get here could wait three more minutes.

You'd be wrong.

Something wasn't right, which it never is. I held back on opening the gate and re-read the manifest again. They were requesting dock for transmitter repair, but that couldn't be the reason they were here. They weren't due to be here. They had a store collection next week, on the same day as Yen Group and Over Group.

I like to get my store collections done on fewer days, to minimise disruption.

No one was due today.

I realised that was the point, at the same moment the system alarms started flashing. Unauthorised access in progress. The system tried to hold them out and I kept my hands off so it could concentrate fully on that.

"Someone is trying to break through the gate," Sap said helpfully.

Me: *Someone is trying to break in.*

Kevan: *Transmitting. I'll try and get someone on the border to contact Marin.*

Me: *They checked-in as usual this morning.*

Asa: *Are you okay?*

Me (vocal): "I'm going into the refuge."

I didn't have time to type my response because the refuge door was triple-locked and that took both hands. It's concealed as a floor tile and I open it once every week. On Mondays. I've never had to use it but I need to know I can and do it quickly. I need to know I won't forget the password. Noa used to say I'd remember the sequence if I needed to, but Noa said a lot of things on which we disagreed.

It took two months before she stopped trying to time her breakfast with mine. She was one of those people who sought out others. A rarity in the Relay Sphere but not unknown – she liked meeting the settlers coming and going, and she requested a colleague. I requested no such thing, but six month's in-situ training is mandatory if you've never left planetside before.

The refuge door slid shut above me. The locations vary by station. They wouldn't be able to find me. Inside the small room I had a limited connection to the system, re-routed through many junctions so they couldn't trace it. There was also a kettle and a small crate of food bars. Noa did the last stock rotation and there were all my favourite flavours.

Kevan: *Are you in?*

Me: *I'm in.*

I pulled up the cameras, but I had to cycle through them one at a time now. The screen in was barely thirty centimetres across and the response time was sluggish. The system threw up blocks as the intruders tried to open the gate.

Sap. I couldn't see Sap. They'd been by the gate. I started cycling through the cameras faster, cursing with each lag. It was like working remotely, on a system on another station, thousands of light-years away, inside a molten moon.

Me: *I can't find Sap.*

Asa: *Are they hiding. They might be hiding.*

Another image flashed in front of me. The storage doors, which Sap had locked. Two figures. That was really all there should be on a Type-C ship, but there was another standing by the gate. They'd all put on coats and pulled up the hoods, so I couldn't see them. It made no difference. The system scanned them, identified them by their chips and pulled up ID cards. I swiped the cards off around the Sphere.

Ute, Paulo, and Matt Marin. They were in their late-teens; brother, sister and a cousin. Matt Marin had shipped through six months ago when he finished at university. I'd let the system process him and he'd stayed in his room until the Type-B came to pick him up.

Me: *They're trying to break into the stores.*

Kevan: *You locked it?*

Me: *I locked it. They can't take the supplies.*

Asa: *Stay put, Paige. Stay where you are.*

Me: *They don't know the system. They'll mess everything up.*

A flash, inside my head. I reached up for the refuge door.

Asa: *Stay put.*

She couldn't see me but I stuck my middle finger up at the stream of text over my wrist and slumped back onto the cushion.

Me: *If I go, I can show them where everything is. They won't break anything.*

Asa: *No.*

Kevan: *What does procedure say?*

I didn't reply. Procedure told me to stay in the refuge unless there was a danger to life. I flipped through the cameras again. They were trying to force the door manually. It crept open and I swiped past. The one by the gate had moved off. Paulo. He was thinner than the other two and had a long stride. He was on the stairs, already past the centre level and halfway to the next. The living quarters.

I threw up more locks in a surge of panic.

My space. Keep out of my space. Out of the empty space that had been Noa's, with her fairy lights and incense sticks and posters of waterfalls. An empty space that echoed. Sap had locked the door after a week and refused to give me the code.

Asa: *Paige, what's happening?*

Me: *They're wandering about. They're going near the living quarters.*

Asa: *Have you found Sap?*

I said no but didn't send it, because I found them. The camera images flashed past as I hammered my finger on the keypad, so when I saw them, I had to flick back. No, no, no. Paulo had found Sap. If I hadn't locked so many doors, the support bot might have found somewhere to hide. Sap made a last skid down a hallway towards the locked-off living quarters before Paulo shot a cable from a tech gun and froze them in their tracks.

Support bots are separate from the system and separate from me. I can't access Sap's systems from the refuge, which would be an unfair thing to do anyway.

Me: *They've got Sap.*

Typing it made my shoulders quiver.

I switched on the sound.

"...is the station's operator?" Paulo asked.

Sap didn't reply.

Asa: *Stay put, Paige.*

Me: *They've got Sap. They're in the stores. They're moving everything. They don't understand how it works.*

It would be quicker if I just went down there and showed them. Ute tossed a crate aside and I flinched.

Ilia (Relay 45): *Paige, what would Noa have done?*

I pulled a face at the text. Noa would probably have gone out there.

Paulo had a metal bar. I hadn't seen it before, carried loose on the opposite side to the camera. He raised it and I flicked away.

Ilia: *How did the low-g exercise go?*

Me: *Sadie won.*

Ilia: *How do you think you can improve on that?*

Me: *I should probably practise more. I keep putting it off. Noa used to remind me.*

Noa thought it was her job to do that, because she was the most experienced and I'd started as her trainee.

Sap.

I reached for the keypad.

Kevan: *I've got Jesh Group here. They're the closest to Marin Group. They'd been looped in on the boost.*

Me: *I can't get through to Marin. Something's wrong with their transmitter.*

It wasn't at my end. I could still get through to everyone else. Comms are the most secure part of a relay station.

Kevan: *Jesh have a trader on Marin right now. There was an abundant tomato harvest.*

Asa: *Jesh need tomatoes?*

Kevan: *They've never been good with warm weather produce. They settled too far north and their world orbits, like, at a snail's pace.*

I knew what they'd say back at Settler Recruitment. Although it's technically fine for someone to operate a relay station solo, your psych eval shows that you benefit from company. It's just a matter of...

Asa: *Paige? Are you still there.*

Me: *I'm here. They're trying to find me.*

I could knock out the systems, perform a reset and catch them while the reboot was in progress. I could suck all the air from the dock. I could...

Asa: *They won't. You know that.*

I found a basic game on the wrist system and started moving little blue crates around. It didn't work. I couldn't concentrate and it wound me up tighter. Even without the cameras I knew they were out there, so I flicked them back on. Seeing what they were actually doing was more calming than my imagination. Paulo was hauling Sap back to the dock and I couldn't tell if he'd managed anything other than to immobilise them.

Kevan: *I've got the Marin Group leader here, via Jesh. They want to talk to you.*

Me: *Well, I don't want to talk to them.*

They were out there, destroying my system and causing general havoc. I'd deny their stock requests forever for this. Marin Group could starve.

Asa: *Yes, you do.*

Me: *I really don't.*

Ilia: *Ok, you don't. But we're not talking to them for you.*

Me: *Vocal?*

Kevan: *You can text if you like. Routing.*

I gripped the edges of my chair.

"Hello? Is that the Relay Station?" I hadn't ever spoken to the Marin Group leader. We communicated via paperwork and basic signals and they'd been out there ten years longer than I'd been in deep space.

Me: *Yes. Relay Station acknowledged. Over.*

"I would like to apologise for what has taken place today. We found the ship missing yesterday and did a roll call. We knew they were missing but we never imagined they would do this."

Me: *You checked in as usual this morning.*

38

"We did not. I imagine they've been intercepting the check-ins. Ute works in communications. Please, route me through to them. They're my siblings' children."

Me: *Why are they doing this? Those supplies are for the other Groups.*

We share equally in Deep Space. To each, according to their need, in a slightly more complicated version of the Basic Survival Allocation on Earth. Freight ships can only carry so much and travel so fast. Once a settler group reaches a certain level of sustainability, they can start putting back in, but so few have reached that yet.

"We don't know. It is unconscionable behaviour. Those supplies will not be welcome back here."

Me: *What about them?*

"They will not be welcomed gladly. Please, let me speak to them."

I had the system do it and while it did, while I let her wait, I reached out again.

Me: *Why would someone take supplies from other settlers?*

Asa: *I don't know.*

Kevan: *It's been fifteen years since anyone tried. I couldn't comprehend it then and I don't now.*

No one else replied. We pondered the impossible question in silence. Those supplies belonged to all of us. They weren't anyone's to take. It just...wasn't the rules. Not rules written on the wall in the centre. The Rules.

"This is Ren Marin. What the hell do you think you're doing?" The Marin leader boomed from the walls of the dock and I routed the comms so the intruders could talk back. Assuming it wasn't a rhetorical question.

"We're taking what's ours," said Paolo Marin. Matt didn't look up from the crate he was carrying. Ute glared at Sap like it was the bot talking.

"Nothing there is yours unless you've requested it."

Matt put the crate down at the gate. "We need these supplies."

"No more than anyone else."

"We never get our fair share. Operator favouritism."

I snapped. What an accusation! "You do. You lying—"

Ren interrupted me. "We get our fair share. If you bring any of those supplies back here, you won't be permitted to land. You can live on them. Don't expect anyone to help you."

"We did this for Marin."

"And Marin tells you, you are doing wrong."

Me: *They said I don't send the supplies out fairly.*

It's the sort of thing incredulous, selfish-minded people say on Earth, about people who decide they'd rather live alone in Deep Space and help people efficiently. Mutterings. There's always mutterings. Noa said that's why she liked to meet the settlers when they came through. Dispel the mutterings.

If I met them, the mutterings would be dispelled with all the efficiency of a megaphone. I know that, however much Noa smiled and said it wasn't true.

Ilia: *We know you do. Everyone knows you do.*

Ada: *You look after your settler groups. We all do. Don't listen to them.*

"This is Grape Jesh, the trade ambassador to Marin Group. We cannot trade with those who steal from us. Think before you do."

I watched on the camera. Sap slid in from the side, picked up the crate Paolo had put down and started back to the store with it. Ute moved aside but Matt lunched forward. He tried to topple the crate.

"That's ours," he shouted.

"It isn't," I said. I wanted them to leave Sap alone to do his job. "I will have Sap load the supplies your group requested in your next shipment. If you go away, I won't report you."

They sulked in a huddle for a moment.

If I reported Marin Group to the Settler Council like I was supposed to, there'd be an inquiry. Everywhere. Of everyone. Maybe even recalls. Very few people were out here because they liked living on Earth.

"We'll take the supplies," said Ute. I think she was in charge.

"Sap," I said. "Please ensure they have the supplies they requested, allowing for fuel allocation."

Type-Cs are designed to fly two passengers and freight, not three. They would need to take some air canisters. I routed the comms back to the refuge.

"This is Ren Marin. I would like to apologise again. I will put in a request for evals as soon as you confirm they've left the Relay. They've been watching shows their cousin brought back. Old shows. The birth-rate is up here and it's been a challenging few years. They thought they were being heroes. We didn't realise it was this serious, and I'm sorry. I should have put in a request earlier. Please don't think Marin doesn't take our settlers' wellbeing seriously."

I didn't know how to respond to that.

Me: *Confirmed. Relay out.*

On the camera, Sap continued to ferry crates, taking their time.

Me: *I think Sap's making them wait on purpose. This will take ages.*

Kevan: *I'd make them wait if I was them.*

Asa: *Are you still in the refuge, Paige?*

Me: *Yes. Can I leave yet?*

Asa: *Stay there until they're gone, I think.*

Kevan: *Better for everyone.*

Me: *Fine.*

I kept the camera on so I could glare at them. That wouldn't do anyone any harm.

Asa: *I've got to go and do some checks. Have you got something you can be getting on with?*

Me: *No.*

Asa: *Nothing?*

Me: *I did the paperwork. I can't do anything else in here.*

Asa: *There must be something. Maybe something you've been putting off.*

41

She signed off. She'd still be there if I wanted, but busy. Slower to reply. There were all the other stations, of course. Thirty people direct and hundreds more in the Sphere. But there was someone else I probably should send a message to. I'd been putting that off. I wanted to wait until it wasn't just one long angry screed, because even I knew anger wasn't fair. No one stayed forever in real life. Nothing lasted.

We'd parted in silence and fury. Her absence still ached.

I swiped the camera off the screen, brought up the long-distance comms hub and the proper keyboard. This was going to need both hands and all my attention.

"Dear Noa. I hope you're enjoying your retirement. I miss you but I'm getting used to the quiet."

I paused as I considered what to say, what to tell this person who had once known everything that happened. That gave me my answer.

"You won't believe what happened today..."

Louise Hughes is a speculative fiction writer from the North East of England. She is also a time traveller, likes to be at the top of mountains, and knits more jumpers than she realistically needs. Her work has appeared in *Strange Horizons, Daily Science Fiction* and *Interzone*.
Louise Hughes is neurodivergent.

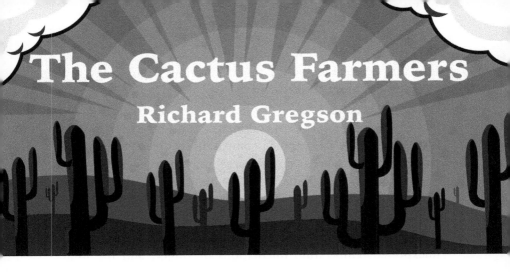

The Cactus Farmers
Richard Gregson

The sun rose over the desert, catching the edges of the roof supports in a liquid russet glow and casting a grid of shadows over the cactus beds beneath. The angular geometric patterns made a stark contrast to the twisted, organic shapes thrown by the prickly pears planted in every second bed down the centre tunnel. Between them, the barrel cactuses squatted in their rows; gnarled, spiky, and indifferent.

I took a mouthful of water and hooked the bottle onto my belt before fishing a breakfast bar out of my pocket. I couldn't bring myself to read the ingredients; the 'new and improved' recipe touted on the wrapper was almost guaranteed to be the same appetizing blend of pasteurized cactus pulp, powdered locust, fake fruit flavour, and just enough sweetener to make it palatable. I peeled back the wrapper and took a bite.

Check that. Almost palatable. Oh well.

The sun lifted clear of the horizon as I chewed on the rest of the bar. I shook myself out of my reverie, washed the sticky grittiness out of my mouth with another swig of water and sat down in front of the computer. I tossed the crumpled wrapper

Art: Adi Kurniawan

into the recycle bin, pulled up the previous night's logs and began paging through them.

To the naked eye, each of Greenhouse One's three tunnels looked much the same as any commercial glasshouse from the last fifty years or so, although their comparatively slender framework would probably have given the game away to an engineer. Like every other modern building, they were riddled with strain gauges, thermocouples, moisture sensors, and everything else that goes into a SmartSuite.

Humidity levels were on the curve, there hadn't been any unexpected temperature fluctuations overnight, and the total collected water figures were squarely average. The pressure sensors told me that the southerly night breeze was beginning to swing around to the west. I tabbed over to the irrigation readouts for the centre tunnel and nodded in satisfaction.

In truth, most of the SmartSuite's capabilities were overkill for a glasshouse, but the water monitoring systems most definitely were not. When every drop of water in the soil had to be accounted for because it was piped in from the local desalination plant, you quickly developed a fine appreciation for your recycling and smart irrigation systems. Forget about spraying water willy-nilly over the beds; each and every barrel or prickly pear in the centre tunnel had its own set of metered micro-dispensers buried next to its roots and hooked up to an electronic management system. Likewise for the dwarf saguaros and the other fruiting cactuses in the right-hand tunnel. The left-hand tunnel ran on a separate closed system – the propagation beds got their own tailored nutrient supply laced with auxins to speed up root development.

I flipped over to the master readouts for the right-hand tunnel and swore out loud. Half of the main schematic was outlined in pulsing red, indicating a blockage or other fault somewhere in the network. A few minutes work isolated the fault to the… *oh great*. It just had to be there, didn't it?

Well, that was my morning gone. I could have waited for Deven, of course, but he wasn't due in till the afternoon shift. According to the manual, I could have left the repairs to him as the senior engineer – the backup systems were there for a reason, and even if they were knocked offline too, the cactuses would survive just fine until we got everything working again. Whether I would survive a day's worth of Deven's patient-but-disappointed looks was another matter.

In Deven's world, you depended on the backups for exactly as long as it took to get the primary systems up and running again, and not a moment longer. I'd never quite dared to ask him whether he learned that the hard way or whether he was just naturally cautious. Either way, he'd been living in this desert since before I was born, so I figured he was probably a good example to follow.

I sighed and hauled out a maintenance cart, dropped my tablet into the pouch on its side, and checked out the tools on the SmartSuite inventory system. I thought for a moment, then palmed open the food locker and retrieved a lunch pack before clipping a rebreather onto my belt. I didn't think Greenhouse One had ever been breached, but there was always a first time and you don't want to be breathing the air outside. Then I began the laborious task of trundling the cart out to the far end of Tunnel Three.

I squinted up at the roof, trying to estimate the time from the sun's position before checking my watch. Another little trick that Deven taught me, although if I ever needed to use it for real then 'running out fast' was likely to be a pretty solid estimate of the time.

The cart wheels squeaked against polished concrete, rumbling over the pipe protectors and cable runs that crisscrossed Tunnel Three's floor. Pushing a cart in here was harder than it looked; whichever way you went, the floor sloped towards a central drain. Great for catching and recycling any spillages; not so great for keeping anything wheeled moving in a straight line. By the time I reached the end of the tunnel, I was breathing heavily, and my arms were definitely beginning to feel the strain. I kicked the wheel locks into place before pulling the workbench out from its slot in the side of the cart and unfolding it. Then I set about isolating the affected cactus beds from the main water supply.

By lunchtime, I'd dug out all the micro-dispensers from beds A through H and had laid them out on the floor on a sheet of polythene. The primary pump sat on the workbench, ready for stripping down. I looked up at the sound of approaching footsteps, wiped the sweat out of my eyes, and waved at Deven. Before handing him my tablet, I cleaned my hands with a squirt of sanitizer gel and dried them on my already mud-streaked towel.

"I already saw the SmartSuite readouts, but thank you. A filter blockage?" It wasn't quite a question.

"Uh-huh. Solid enough that the backflush cycle tripped a fault last night." I watched him page through the system faults on my tablet.

"And you intend to clean the pump and dispensers as a precaution?" Another not-quite question.

"Yup. I don't think there's anything wrong with them but..."

"You want to double check. Very good." Deven's lips twitched in amusement at my carefully neutral expression. "I may yet make an engineer of you, but for now, I believe it is lunchtime. Thorough work requires a..."

"Full stomach," I finished, my own stomach suddenly growling in agreement. "I hear you, boss." I put my tools back in their caddy, fished out my lunch pack, and sat down on the edge of one of the cactus beds. Deven arranged himself cross-legged on the floor, his movements stiffer than I remembered. I studied him for a moment, noting the age spots on the back of his hands and the deep-set wrinkles around his eyes. His short-cropped salt-and-pepper hair seemed greyer than I remembered, standing out against his leathery, dark brown skin.

Turning away before he noticed me staring, I tore open my lunch pack and regarded the oval loaf of pumpernickel-dark bread without enthusiasm. I broke off its top and inspected the lumpy, brownish-yellow contents, my nose wrinkling at the smell. Spooning up a mouthful of the slop with the loaf end, I waited for the inevitable chilli burn and was pleasantly surprised when my tongue failed to ignite. I read the list of ingredients on the wrapper, swallowing my mouthful before looking up. "They're spoiling us this week. Soya, mushroom, and actual dehydrated potato."

Deven raised his eyebrows. "A new and improved recipe?"

"Aren't they always? This one is almost edible though."

"A pleasant change." Deven broke open his own ration pack and snapped the top off his own loaf. "Yes, indeed. Almost edible. No more than thirty percent crushed insect, I would say."

We finished our lunch in companionable silence. Deven brushed the last few crumbs off his beard, climbed to his feet, and eyed the assorted components laid out on the floor. "How much progress have you made with the cleaning?"

I stood up and tossed my lunch wrapper in the recycler. "I hadn't yet. The stripping down took me all morning."

"In that case, if you don't mind, I will dismantle and clean the pump and filters, while you attend to the micro-dispenser tubing. I'll find it easier to work on my feet."

"Sure." I busied myself unclipping the air duster from the side of the cart, unwilling to meet his eyes. I plugged it in and began cleaning out the dispensers while Deven picked up a screwdriver and turned his attention to the pump casing.

The work was a frustrating combination of repetitive enough to be tedious but fiddly enough not to be relaxing. Dismantle dispenser, test sensors and valve, blow out tubing and nozzle head with air duster, hook up to water supply on cart, run flow test. Repeat with the next dispenser. I was most of the way through the pile when a peculiarly fetid smell rolled over me, almost making me gag. "Whew – you found the blockage then?"

Deven grunted. "And I'll dispose of it through the macerator. I don't believe this will benefit our grow beds."

"Not if that smell is anything to go by. Man, but that's a ripe one." I heard the distinctive rustle of a compost bag, and the stench relented slightly. "No wonder the backflush wigged out."

"Indeed. Have you found any blockages in the dispensers?"

"Nothing that the air duster couldn't dislodge."

"Good." Deven walked over and inspected the pile of cleaned components. "I'll have finished the last filter unit by the time you're finished." He glanced at the sky. "We should have enough time left to rebuild the system before the end of the shift."

He was right – having two pairs of hands to re-plant the dispenser grids made everything else go a lot faster. The outside lights were just starting to come on as we ran the final diagnostics on the newly reinstalled pump. Deven nodded in satisfaction as, one by one, the red warning lights on my tablet blinked out. I watched him unlock the tool cart's wheels and heave it around, trying to hide my concern at the trembling in his arms. I should have known better.

"It was difficult to maintain my exercise regime from a hospital bed."

I stepped forward, one hand reaching out to help, only to pull up short at the expression on Deven's face. The irregular squeaking of rubber on concrete broke the silence and I fell in beside him as he began pushing the cart back to its storage rack. I studied my tablet for a moment, unable to meet my mentor's eyes. "So how was..."

"The hospital? They looked after me well and they don't think I'll need to go back again."

I blew out my cheeks in relief. "That's fantastic news!" A sudden chill ran down my spine. "Isn't it? You don't need to go back because the treatment worked, right?"

"My final scan was clear. The last T-cell infusion was a success, it seems."

I grinned foolishly. "Score one for modern biotech!"

"Modern engineering," Deven corrected me with a faint smile. "Genetic engineering is still engineering."

I was too happy to argue. "A few weeks at the gym to get over the bed rest, and you can think about booking your ticket home!" I paused. "Maybe more than a few weeks. Recovering from cancer and all that."

"Indeed." Deven fell silent for a moment. "I asked about the journey home before I left the hospital. The doctors did not recommend it." His voice took on the clipped tones that I associated with technical briefings. "The radiation risk is high given my age, and my oncology and immunology profiles are both lower-quartile. Hence there is a non-trivial likelihood that I will develop another cancer type. If I do so, then I am a less than optimal candidate for further T-cell treatments and will probably be reliant on medium specificity chemotherapy."

Oh. I bit my lip, feeling the happiness draining out of me. "That's rough, boss. Really rough, I mean."

"Yes, I thought so too to begin with." Deven stared up at the darkening, butterscotch-coloured sky, which was just beginning to fade into the blue of sunset. "But I've been thinking about it a lot. After all, it is not so long ago that people would have been envious of me spending the rest of my days here." He pointed. "And even now, there are not so many people who have seen that."

I looked up, my gaze following the direction of his finger. A line of three evening stars reached towards the horizon, two white and one azure. Phobos and Deimos – fear and terror – pointing the way to Earth. An all-too-apt metaphor, I thought, for my friend's abandoned journey. I lowered my eyes and stared out across the Martian desert, lit by a last sliver of daylight. "No. There are worse places to spend the rest of your life."

Richard Gregson lives in Bathgate, Scotland and works for a Scottish biotech company as an intellectual property manager. A previous job at a crop research facility provided inspiration for the setting of *The Cactus Farmers*.

The Anchoress

Maya Chhabra

now

When I die, I will not rot. I will travel onward.

The capsule that contains my body will continue falling through space, with no one to see out of the portal into the mysteries of the universe as I get closer and closer to the heart of things. And one – *day* has no meaning here – some time, I will burn in flame.

That is my godless credo.

then

Before the bishops would let me do it, they examined me for mental illness. Cardinals interrogated me about my calling, tore me to shreds. The Pope himself, in a private audience, told me I would be forgiven if I changed my mind, unlike the olden days when escaped religious were brought back by force. I think he wanted to dissuade me.

But how could they forbid me? What God was telling me to do had precedent: Julian of Norwich, the countless anchorites of the Middle Ages. The tradition had lived into the 20th century

– a nun had gone into such seclusion in 1945 – then sputtered out.

Until me.

I was young, and fervent, and capable of deceiving myself that I was humble. They did their best, the hierarchs of the Church, to pierce that humility and discover if it was a lie. But even I did not know I was lying. I burned for sacrifice, for holiness, for God.

They sealed me into the spaceship, all fire and light. I was to pray for the universe in my tiny cell. It had a sort of portal, a hagioscope, through which I might admire God's handiwork, and a radio in case something went truly wrong.

now

It still has a portal.

then

For two years, I prayed in peace. The routine was much like the convent, though without my sisters. Their absence tugged at me like gravity once had. But I offered that up to heaven. And what a heaven!

I saw Saturn's rings, counted them one by one, lost myself in the ever-finer gradations. God's playfulness, his joy on full display in this pointillist miracle. Dust and rock turning to monumental beauty. I thought, surely I am blessed.

I was closer to God than I had ever been or would be again. For after the capsule passed Saturn, something changed.

now

I keep much the same routine as before; the same freeze-dried meals, the same hours. I use a twenty-four-hour clock, as if at home. I stare, sometimes, at the broken radio, but I try not to brood. I stare out of the portal, and record observations no one will ever read. I am sane, I think.

then

It started as a mere distraction, a dust mote in my vision. What if I had been wrong? What if it wasn't God calling me to do this, but my own hubris?

Over time, I worsened. Doubt clawed at me like a devil in my breast, like a teething baby demanding to be fed. Sometimes I wanted to claw myself, to ease the pain in my mind.

Where was God? And why could he not save me from myself?

I could not pray without the unwanted thought pinwheeling at the edge of my attention: *what if it's not true? What if you've sealed yourself away for a lie?*

I was proud, for all that pride was a sin. I could not bear the idea of being a dupe. But if I had deceived myself, there was only one way forward. I had to call for help.

It would be a humiliation – the only anchoress in centuries giving up after two short years when she had pledged a lifetime. And I could not bring myself to do it. If I still believed, I could bear the humiliation. Had Christ not borne worse for my sake?

But I doubted, and remained silent.

now

Today we are passing a nursery of stars. If I had control over the spaceship's steering computer, I would plunge myself into those columns of stardust. But I do not control where I go.

The thing about taking a leap of faith is that if no one catches you, you are always falling.

then

Outside the solar system, far from the grasp of the sun, I began to doubt my sanity as well. *Nothing can cut you off from God's love*, I told myself, but I had cut myself off from everything. The radio ate away at my peripheral vision; it was always there.

I prayed, numb and lost. No answer came. A dark night of the soul, a thing that happened even to saints. But if – if there was simply no one … and then the growing horror. What had I condemned myself to?

I could bear this if I had You.

now

I have come to the end of my pride. Today I will try to repair the radio. The hardest part is not fiddling with the miniature pieces. The hardest part is hope.

Because what if I can't do it? What if I really am stuck here till I die? I will not even have the satisfaction of not even trying to avoid my fate.

then

Choice was driving me mad. I had thought I had no more choices, once I sealed myself away, believed I had given that all up. But one option remained. The silent radio tormented me.

I could hear a human voice again. I could leave. I did not have to do this.

And the more I fought to keep on, the more I hated God. Pride was all that sustained my faith now, and that still small voice told me not to listen to it.

What do you want? I asked into the night. It was always night, always starlight. *What do you want from me?*

A great release of tension, as if someone I did not realise was holding me, had released his grip.

now

There is a part I cannot find, the original tiny microphone whose replacement doesn't work. It must be somewhere in here, for there is nowhere else. But I have not seen it floating in my cell, and there is nowhere it could have fallen. Maybe it is broken, too. Wherever it is.

Even my tears stick to my face, the occasional drop escaping into the air.

I will live here all the rest of my life, and I will always know now that I am a coward.

then

The death rattle of belief was ringing in my ears like tinnitus. I could not pay attention to anything. I could not hear anyone. That was the condition I was in two years ago, when I made my decision.

I had to call for help. There was nothing else to be done.

I brought out a tool kit in case something needed fixing. After all, the radio had never been used.

My trembling fingers held down the button. I heard the static crackle, the start of something that might have been a voice.

And I let go. Grabbed the heavy wrench. Began to break the radio, ripping out its innards, tearing the wires, smashing the components. Some I couldn't break; those I scattered.

Now I had no more choices. Now I had pledged myself utterly. Now I had to believe.

I had flung myself into God's arms. But there was nothing there. I passed through them, and kept falling.

now

If I don't get up to look for the microphone, no one will ever have to know. And if no one knows, is it real? If only God knows you don't believe in him...but the paradox eludes me, floating away like the stray teardrops.

I grab the netting on the wall so that I won't bump my head or hurt myself while I can not see properly, cannot breathe. Something small and hard pops through the coarse rope. I reach out and grasp for it, sending myself hurtling into the opposite wall.

When I look back, and the stars in my vision clear, it is still there. The little microphone, appearing the very moment I need it. I thought once that there were no coincidences. I am not so sure, now. But every now and then, I doubt even my doubt.

then

Grace was not a thing you earned by being good enough. That had been drummed into me since my novitiate. Didn't the absence of grace mean the opposite, then? It was all the more important to accept the consequences of one's choices, to not cast about desperately for some mean escape, some way out.

That was what held me back. The fear of escaping. The idea repelled me, turned my stomach, even as it tempted. It offended my pride.

So much for my humility. Solitude had revealed this much to me, at least: what hung between me and salvation.

now

It has been years since I smashed the radio, but there it is. The thing I need. It floats in front of me like a hallucination or a miracle. I have only to reach out and take it.

Maya Chhabra is the author of a children's novel, Stranger on the Home Front, as well as short stories and poetry in *Strange Horizons, PodCastle*, and *Daily Science Fiction*, among other venues. She has a YA verse novel forthcoming in 2022. She lives in New York with her wife.

A Flight of Birds

E.M. Faulds

I'm hungry. How long are you supposed to leave it between feedings anyway? The question floats above my head every now and then; a scribbly little black cartoon cloud with lightning bolts and knives stabbing out of it. For a cloud, it's heavy. It stands up against the fug of the coffee house as the espresso machine gently farts and hisses disapprovingly at my side. I'm hungry. But, more importantly, Jimmy's late.

I lean low over the counter, check the light levels through the steamed-up glass frontage behind Mr Chowdhury. The space around the black and orange curlicue font decals is still dark. No need to panic, yet. He sips from the tiny cup of cortado that he takes after his shift at the all-night newsagent and rustles a paper with the headline 'Police Baffled'. We never talk while he's sitting. It suits us both that way – he likes to wind down and I don't like talking too much. It shows my teeth. Don't worry, I'd never bite him. Then there'd be no-one in here for large swathes of time and that would be worse than the hunger. And besides, he's silent, but it's the good kind, the amiable kind. I don't think he's ever hurt anyone in his life. But the world outside the coffee shop? That's a different story.

Byres Road, West End, Glasgow. This time of night it's nose-to-tail parked cars. Cycle back a couple of hours and it's jumping, filled with entrepreneurs talking about engagement dynamics on their way to a craft beer popup, managing directors pushing past students in the plethora of vegan cafes, bus after bus, drunkards struggling back to the subway after the work's night out, or the people so lost in their lives they can only express themselves through a ragged, existential yawp. And I get to deal with them all on a nightly basis. But from now until end of shift, it's Monday-night quiet. Morning will come and the machine winds up again until all you can hear is the buzz of people and the rumble-shake of the train tunnel under your feet. Not that I get to see that.

04:30. A time etched onto the leathery surface of my heart. It's the earliest the sun ever rises in Glasgow. If I'm not home that time around the solstice, I've got drama coming. By July, August, there's some play. Two extra minutes of darkness every morning. A wee buffer if it's raining, which it usually is. By winter, I'm golden. Some days it's as if the sun just doesn't bother. But it's May, the sunniest weather, and I've got to be careful.

The angry growls of hunger in my stomach are making me obsess-spiral. As far as I know, there's no reason to worry.

Don't get me wrong, I don't want to kill anybody, but my urge to bite is rubbing at me like sandpaper. It's a pain that never goes away. Neither do the cold fingers, even now in summer. I'm reliably informed it gets roasting in here when the espresso machines are going full bore in the middle of a July day, but I'll not get to find that out. I told Scott I was studying palaeontology at Uni so I could never do daytimes, always had to be out the door by 04:00 at the latest. He never wondered when exactly I'd sleep, and I only have to endure the occasional quiz about what the best dinosaur is. ("Well, you see Scott, the more you learn about them, the more you realise they're all special in their own way.") And the nickname DG. For "Dino-girl".

Mr Chowdhury brings back his wee cup and saucer with a smile. His neat moustache has a little smoosh of froth on it, but I don't want to embarrass him. "Goodnight, darling, or should I say good morning?" He always makes the same joke and always calls me darling because he thinks it's a nice thing to say to a woman. I tell him I'll see him tomorrow and he's off home.

I'm alone again for a while, only the wall-clock and the espresso machine's conversation with itself marking time. I wonder what's waiting for Mr Chowdhury at home. A quiet, sleeping household of warm beds? A bare mattress in a flat above the shop? The ghost of cooking clinging to the soft furnishings or a wreckage of take away containers? You never know what goes on in someone else's home. And I can never get close enough to ask.

The vanishing people. That's what they should call us. Hotel staff, refrigerated lorry drivers, bartenders, office cleaners, alkies, call centre workers, cops, and robbers. People who vanish from the daytime world's consciousness. We may as well not exist as far as they're concerned. But we exist for each other. There's recognition in their eyes, relief when they see there's space and peace here for them. And they have absolutely no idea what they mean to me.

A baobhan sith's never born. They're made. My maker was some old prick in Queen's Park who lurched out of the bushes. I thought he was just a homeless person off his face on Buckie, so put my black belt in Taekwondo to good use and sent him back into the bushes. But before he disappeared, I got a scratch off one of his teeth on my little finger. Not a bite. Not a sensual clinch of neck nibbling that looks pure like sex. No, a bit of a tear. I've had worse cuts making a sandwich. And that was it.

Adrenaline and shock made me go to the out-of-hours clinic at the Victoria, but they just gave me a bandage and stuck my arm with a needle the size of a drinking straw, "Just to be sure." I didn't bother going to the police. I told the medical staff it had been an accident. What was I going to say? That I'd kicked a homeless guy in the baws?

I went home. It was there, tucked up in my own bed, that the wrongness came down on me.

A long time later, I cottoned on to the fact it's not just passed on to anybody. That there has to be something else. Something inside you that says, *enough*.

There are customers who come in during the wee hours that don't fit the late-night crowd so neatly. Like her. She works both days and nights, gets to walk both sides of Glasgow's darkness and light. I don't know her, but she comes in wearing purple scrubs and orders one of those coffee cups as big as your heid. She sits at a small table by the power sockets, typing on her laptop for up to three hours. Sometimes she's there as I come on shift, sometimes as I'm about to go off. I know the name on her debit card is Miss C. Thompson. Whatever the 'C' stands for, she doesn't look like she wants to be a Cathy or a Claire, fingers thumping at the keyboard so fast it's like a hailstorm on a garden shed. Maybe a Charlotte or a Cordelia, maybe a Celeste. It's one of those initials that can swing right through the spectrum from hard to soft. But I just think of her as C.

In the intricate daydreams I have during a shift, C knows all about my condition. She's constantly pestering me to come forward and share my condition with science and get on the telly and I have to regretfully refuse, saying, "I work best in darkness." In reality, I know exactly the face she would put on. Right before she told me not to make such a stupid joke.

It's 04:45. Jimmy still hasn't come in to take the early shift. He hasn't replied to my texts and I'm getting antsy. The details of the street outside are far too crisp; the sliver of sky above the shops opposite has gone from navy to steel blue. C's still here, and the apprentices have drifted in for their triple-shot Americanos – showing off, bless 'em. I want to kick them all out and shut up shop, but I don't think I'd have a job tomorrow if I did. And he said he'd be here.

"C'mon, Jimmy," I mutter and jiggle from one foot to the other. I'm so twitchy I hardly notice that C is staring at me. She has earbuds but they must have been down low. Or she's using the trick where she just puts them in her ears to keep people away.

She takes one of the headphones out.

"Sorry," I say, finally clocking her. "Talking to myself."

She smiles and nods awkwardly. "Sorry, I thought you were speaking to me."

I mean, yes, that's obvious. "Sorry, no. No." This could go on all night. I want it to stop but it's like a car crash. I watch the words fall out of my mouth. "Just wondering where my colleague has got to." Why do I do that? Just say no and leave it at that.

"Is your shift over?" she asks.

C, please stop.

"Yup." Me, please stop, you're no good at this. You were never good at this. Always on the periphery of conversations, back when you had a group of pals to hang out with. Walking between pubs on a night out, you'd always manage to fall between the twos and threes who were chatting arm in arm. And even those days are just a Vaseline-smeared lens of memory, now.

"Are you going to miss your bus or anything?" She's still poised with that earbud halfway out, tentative. Like a deer on the edge of a forest. I guess she can see the stress lines I get on my forehead. Or how I'm nearly dancing on the balls of my feet. "I could give you a lift maybe?"

"It's okay, I can walk, it's not too far."

"Are you sure?" C, I'm begging you. Please stop, you're killing me with awkwardness, and I'm basically immortal.

"No, it's fine," I smile, a closed-lips tight little smile. "I could use the exercise. Thanks, though."

The badness. The wrongness. It came over me while I lay in bed trying to shake off the jitters after the prick in the park attacked me. I hate confrontation, spent most of my life trying to avoid it. I'm not a coward, mind. And I have a black belt in TKD. That's not easy to do. But confrontation rattles me, it takes me ages after to stop chewing it over and over. Like, how dare he? Should I have gone to the polis? I was staring at the strips of light and shadow on my ceiling, playing it over in my head, when it came down.

How to explain it? Have you ever seen that video of the deep-sea footage of a giant squid? It looms out of the black, bobs and dances for a while, caresses the camera equipment with its tentacles and drifts off. Then it comes back like a reverse explosion, all its arms pointed together like a knife and at the last second, they lunge and wrap and that's the end of the recording.

That. It's like that.

I have to ring Scott and he comes in. Jimmy's getting fired, I can tell that much by his face. "Thanks, DG," he tells me and says he'll put the extra time on my wages. I barely take the time to nod as I hang up my apron and scramble a hoody on. I've got about fifteen minutes to get half an hour across town.

I'd duck into the subway, but it won't be open for another hour. I like it down there when it's quiet. It's the safest place I could be in the daytime but it's more than that. The sound of the train is loud but that just means hardly anyone bothers talking and you can retreat into your own little world while the carriage rocks you back and forth. The stations smell like wet stone and metal, and I can't tell you why I like that, but I do.

Today, though, I have to run. I dig sunglasses out of my pocket. I'm already wearing trainers, but I've been on my feet for six hours and my backpack is full of junk that juggles about and digs into my kidneys. I consider a bus, but the routes are wrong, they'll take too long. I head down towards the river. I can follow it back to Finnieston, scarper across the bridge at the SECC.

If I could live in the West End, I would. But it's as possible for me as flying, which, no. I can't.

I try to keep to the shadows at the foot of the row of shops but soon the disadvantage of living south of the river hits me, quite literally, in the face. I pull my hood forward as far as it'll go, but it's not quite enough.

I remember blundering into the sunlight when I was just new. I mean, it really hadn't sunk in. I wasn't thinking, walked smack bang into broad daylight. Not for long, mind, but long enough.

There's no baobhan sith support group to tell you what to do. I didn't even know what I was. I thought it was classic vampirism all the way, the Bela Lugosi stuff. To be fair, a lot of it basically works the same. But Scotland's always had a history of blood-drinkers. True, the folklore that accreted around it is mostly wrapped up in transparently sexist bullshit.

Some men go get pished in a little isolated hut, a shieling. They start dancing, just for fun. They make the mistake of wishing for some female company and all of a sudden there's a knock on the door. A sexy lady appears. One of the men notices she has the feet and legs of a deer, so instead of warning his pals that something is up, he legs it. So, of course, Mr Lucky is the only survivor, as the rest are massacred, their throats laid open. He says it was a baobhan sith that did it and he was spared her attack because he was the only virtuous one among the group.

People believed what they wanted to back then, didn't they?

Baobhan sith means: the human plus package – not quite super-strength, but tough, not a lot going on in the heartbeat department, a shocking sunlight allergy, an outsize desire to drink blood. Tick in each of those columns. No deer feet. And no get out of jail free card for lying wee shites like the guy in the story.

Quite the opposite.

I slam through the door of the close and take the stairs two or three at a time. When I'm safe in the flat, I strip off and rush to the bathroom to sit in the tub, spraying my face with the shower hose attachment on cold.

I get out after about half an hour, inspect the damage in the bathroom cabinet mirror. (Yes, I have a reflection. If photons could pass through me, UV light wouldn't be so bloody problematic, would it?) I look like what I am – a burns victim. It's mostly confined to my cheeks and chin, some of my wrists where they weren't deep enough in my pockets. Even with the hoody and my head down, the light bounced off the pavement. Without the sunnies, I guess my eyelids would have welded shut. I touch the tender area with my fingertips and some of the top layer sloughs off with a cut-glass pain. I can't even scream because it'd stretch my lips, so I end up clenching my jaw and mewling like a kitten.

I think about calling Scott to see if I can take tonight off, but I doubt he'll let me if Jimmy got bounced from the rota. I creak the cabinet open, tired, and get the tube of aloe vera.

It takes a couple of hours of lying still, coating myself in green gel and holding a bag of frozen peas to my face while at the same time trying not to touch it at all. I don't heal per se. But the pain stops being so insistent after a while. The skin will stop peeling soon, just look like a huge rashy sunburn, which will fade back to the regular anaemic pallor eventually. But for now, I have to wait, lying here, listening to the world wake up and get on with it on the other side of my blackout curtains while I weather the pain. I want to go to sleep but every time I do, some wanker bangs the close door or beeps a horn. Every sound is too sharp, layering on top of the burns. Eventually, I grit my teeth and get out my phone for something to do. Open up Fotousi and scroll through the posts of accounts I follow. Nothing great. A few interesting ones from @mejer_playa, but it feels crap having nothing to post of my own. I try to put something up every day. Gives me that little buzz when someone likes a pic, Pavlov's dog that I am. And it feels like connection, even if it's not really real.

My account is all shots, (unsurprisingly), of the nightlife in Glasgow. I had to save up to buy my handset outright since my credit rating is so crap. But it takes the best low-light pictures. I scroll back through my own timeline, tasting each moment. It might be egotistical, but I like what I did, or I wouldn't do it. Pictures of people spilling out of bars under smeared neon and bokeh string lights; the Mitchell Library like a parliament house, a Tiffany lamp knockoff in a wee oval window in a pebbledash council house wall. I even once caught a bunch of lads making a human pyramid to put the traditional hat on the head of the statue of Wellington. I hadn't really thought how it was done before; the orange and silver traffic cone just appeared, like a snowdrop in the spring.

I should get over to the Necropolis. I promised myself a photoshoot there on a dead night. A quiet night. Just me. And the goths finger-banging up against a mausoleum, but I could work around them. Good view from the top of the hill.

I found him again. The one who bit me.

I put two and two together after the wrongness had cleared. At the time, I'd thought it was the flu. You know the type where you can barely get out of bed to pee, barely hold down fluids? Turns out it wasn't that. When I finally let myself comprehend what was going on, that I was dead but still, you know, *continuing*, I thought I might find him. When I regained my strength. To my surprise, I had a lot more strength than before. It didn't make up for being relegated to the dark, segregated from the rest of humanity, but it was useful.

I spent a lot of nights hanging out in the bushes at Queen's Park, tempted to leap out and drag some people back into the shadows myself.

But I didn't. Knowing that the urge could be resisted just made me angrier. He came along the path, looking at joggers going by, and I knew. Knew it was him. Funny thing was, he didn't even see what he'd done. He wasn't a baobhan sith, just a carrier. Just a sad fuck who preyed on people for his own thrills. Admitted to attacking girls, kids sometimes. He let that slip when I had him up against a wall two feet off the ground.

I'm not too proud of what came after.

The shop door goes and there's the *swipp* of corduroyed thighs and the clack of summer shoes as someone crosses the floor. I know before turning my head that it's C, early tonight. She's wearing a light peasanty blouse with paisley print in green, brown cords and flat sandals. Her nose, cheeks, and neckline are almost as red as my face beneath my full-coverage foundation. I guess she had a day off, maybe sat out in Kelvingrove on the grass bit where everyone ignores the outdoor drinking ban and brings a disposable barbecue. But now she's here, and there's her laptop bag. "The usual," she says, dimpling.

Number seven brew, venti latte. "I'll bring it over," I tell her as she blips her debit card.

"Cheers," she says and goes to set up her laptop. I've never managed to see what she's writing. She sits with her back to the wall. I hope it's not sparkly vampire fic.

Although, that would be something to talk about.

I used to have family. My dad hit my mum, but she wouldn't leave him, though I begged her. So, I left instead, went to Glasgow, flat shared and took shitty jobs until I could save up for a place of my own. I found some friends and I was going to make something of my life. It makes me really tired thinking about all this stuff. But yeah, I'd found a new life. And then the guy in the park, the cut on my pinkie.

How could I explain what was going on? To anyone? "Oh, by the way, I'm kind of like a vampire but more tartan"? I fobbed them off with excuses, was sarcastic, withering, utterly horrible. Until they stopped messaging. I burned my old accounts. My Fotousi handle is just a random string of letters. I don't really know why I bother with it. I guess it gives the illusion of not being alone.

I take the bus up towards the cathedral on my way to work on the Tuesday night, so I can do my photoshoot but get to my shift in good time. I hang on to a pole with my back to the bag rack and don't look anybody in the eye. I'm not unusual-looking enough to raise a comment. No deer feet or anything. Only, I'm female for all eternity.

I can see one of the passengers nudging his pal and pointing at me. He thinks he's being subtle. He hasn't got a handle on how peripheral vision works. I turn my shoulder as if I'm looking out the window, to put my arm as a barrier between them and my tits. (Well, what else am I going to do? On a bus?) Soon as I can, I ding the bell and scoot up to the cobbled precinct. The black spire of the cathedral pokes up into the dark denim blue of the summer night sky.

They have a gate and opening hours, which is sweet. As if it would stop any moderately determined Glaswegian. I hop the low fence at the side of the manse and get out my phone as I check around for other night-time visitors. A lot of kids come up here, trying to be edgy.

Movement. A fox trots out between the gravestones and off on his own business. He's too quick for me to get a shot. I turn the screen brightness right down on my phone and head for the path up the hill. Saints and draperies, baroque mausoleums and palatial tombs, statues to the rich and powerful. I wonder if any of the Tobacco Lords are buried with a stake through the heart.

There's a tiny rotunda that sits proud of the hillside not far from the Knox monument which I climb up to park myself, back to the base of a column. There are still the dregs of a sunset off the way I came, just a glow where the sun ducks under the horizon. I guess I'm lucky I don't live in the north, up Orkney way. Or Lapland.

I raise my phone and open the camera app, steady my elbows on my knees and start taking pictures: a Victorian angel's outstretched hand in silhouette. Moss growing out of a small spire. A tree elbows its way between graves, knocking them sideways in extreme slow motion while little birds dart in and out of the dark mass of leaves. Summertime and they don't really know what to do with themselves. A dawn chorus that barely ends. How quiet must they feel in the long winter nights, the ones who stay, the ones who don't get to fly south? Not on the cards for me either, birds.

I'm aware of the two people staggering up the path beneath the rotunda a long time before they get here. The giggles and loud shushing of people drunk enough to think they're being quiet. She's holding onto his elbow but keeps going over on her ankles. I put my phone away and stay still as a gargoyle. It's easy for me. They don't notice. The guy is playing along, but I can see he's a lot less pished than she is. He's glancing sharply at the shadows. Not looking where I'm sitting above their heads.

She's middle aged and middle class. He's unremarkable. Remarkably unremarkable. He shoves her down on the grass. She's stunned at first. Laughs, thinks they fell over. Then she makes some confused 'what are you doing?' type noises.

I hop down from the rotunda and when I'm behind him, as he's fiddling with his zipper and trying to cover her mouth, I shout "Oi!"

He jerks his head around. His eyes are deader than mine. When he sees I'm a woman he says, "Fuck off, this is none of your business."

"I'm calling the polis," I say, loudly.

He ignores me. He knows by the time they come it'll be too late.

It's time for me to do the thing. I don't want to do the thing. But for him, I will.

I was always told women should never go out at night in Glasgow on their own. Never take a shortcut down the lanes, make sure to get in a registered taxi, make sure you can kick your heels off and run if you need it. Now I go to the dark corners, the unlit paths on purpose. What's shocking? The amount of crime that isn't reported.

I go towards the muffled struggle these days. I've got it down to a fine art. The one being held down only knows it's stopped, thinks the bad guy was scared off. It happens so quick they can't tell that it's me. Can't thank me. What I do isn't legal, and it isn't nice. I try not to do it if I can help it. And I don't like the idea of someone not facing a jury for what they did. But, at the same time, I have to feed and it isn't pretty. In fact, I kind of have to make it messy to cover up the marks.

I'm sure some of Police Scotland suspect there's a vampire in Glasgow. But they'd never say that out loud, in public.

I haven't met any other baobhan sith. I think I'd know them. I knew the one who turned me, figured out he was a carrier, but I've never had a reaction to anyone else. I'd love to meet one. Then they could tell me what the fuck I'm supposed to do with the rest of my life. Or unlife. Whatever. I mean, tearing the throats out of scumbags is something I'm good at, but it's not a *career*, you know?

And I wouldn't be so alone.

She's sobbing uncontrollably because she feels stupid. I'm holding her up so I can walk her down to somewhere safe. She's fighting the alcohol but it's winning. I don't normally let them see me, but I can't leave her here, vulnerable. And I don't think she'll be able to identify me. Her eyes aren't focusing right.

"It's okay," I say, over and over. I try to ask her if she wants to go to the police.

"He said we should go watch the sunrise," she replies. "I thought he was being romantic." She vomits copiously on her shoes. In my bag next to the balled-up, blood-soaked wet wipes, I have a little packet of tissues. I give her one. She dabs it vaguely near her lips.

I have to get to work, so I see her to the taxi rank down where the streets are well lit. I make a point of hearing her tell the driver where she lives while I take pictures of his plates. He won't try anything. I don't think she says thank you, but I really don't want her to. I keep thinking about who will find the body stuffed into that niche in the mausoleum and hate myself.

I jog to work, holding my belly as it sloshes. My physical health appreciates it, if not my spiritual.

"Good night, darling, or rather, good morning," Mr Chowdhury says. Tomorrow his paper will say 'Urban Foxes Attack Deceased in Grisly Find' or something. People always find a way to explain what they don't want to think about. I wave and give him a solemn nod while I upload the photos of the birds to Fotousi. Those were the best of the night, before I had to break off. The shutter speed was slow, so they streak and zoom out of the tree like dark thoughts, the threat of daylight looming behind them, just over the horizon. No flying south.

Square it up, filters? Naw, it's good as is. I post and put the phone down under the counter, beside the glass latte mugs. It's quiet in the shop tonight except for C's keyboard storm, punctuated by moments where she leans back and scrolls on the mousepad with one hand and holds her huge coffee cup with the other. She clicks and her eyebrows plunge and then she snorts and smiles and clicks some more. Then back to the words.

Scott left a note on the whiteboard in the 'staff room', (a big cupboard where you can hide pretending to look for extra filters). On the board, the rotas get thrashed out. The column under the letter 'J' has been scribbled out with furious marker strokes. Then, 'DG – extra shifts?' He wants me to do more work. I wonder if he's going to try to add to my responsibilities. I'll tell him if I'm late again I'll shut up the shop. I'll say there's a relative I'm caring for. Something no-one would argue with. I get my phone out to look up obscure geriatric medical terms. Can't be too careful. He's the type to go check there really is such a thing as an Ankylosaurus.

A Fotousi notification appears on my screen: *Cassandra Thompson hearts your photograph.* I check the avatar on the account. It's her. It's C.

She's bringing her empties back to the counter. My first instinct is to hide the phone back under the counter. She doesn't know it's me. She can't. My face and name are nowhere to be seen on the Fotousi wall. There is no trail, I've made sure of that. But she looks up from balancing the cups. She sees my face. "What's up? You all right?"

I deflect. "Yeah, just funny. I..." It's easier to just show her so I shove the screen over before I can think carefully. She sees the app, my account, the photo, her heart.

Her mouth hangs open and I know the next word out of her mouth will be 'stalker', or 'weirdo', but it's not. "What are the chances?" She shifts her laptop bag onto her shoulder better.

"You working to fund your artistic endeavours, too?" She nods at the apron, the espresso machine.

I shrug. "Naw… photography's just a hobby." I sound so useless I want to die. Except I can't. Did that already.

"Oh, you should do something with it. It's important. Art helps people. Brings them together. And you're really good." She looks vaguely towards the door. "I have to go, get some sleep. I'm on shift in three hours again." Lates then earlies? That's tough. I reach for her tray, but she pins me with her eyes. With her dimples. "But let me know if you're ever doing an exhibition. Or selling prints. I'd love to be your first customer."

"Th-thanks, that's very kind." I can't help but answer her grin before I remember myself and cover my teeth with my hand. She gives me a look that's puzzled but kind.

"Not at all," she says and pats the counter in farewell as she heads out.

The tingles last all the way to the end of shift. I walk home. Birds are zooming about, dark streaks against a denim-blue sky, and my Converse about two feet above the pavement. I might be getting ahead of myself, but maybe there's something to the idea of having friends. They can see stuff when you're oblivious. Believe in you when you think you're hopeless.

Maybe I'll try again. I'll do everything different this time.

E.M. Faulds is an Australian who now calls Scotland home. She lives not far from Glasgow, in the oldest house in town. She has written a novel, *Ada King*, and created and hosted the British Fantasy Award nominated podcast, *Speculative Spaces*. She also edited and contributed to *Flotation Device*, a charity anthology for the Glasgow SF Writers' Circle, of which she is a member. Follow her on Twitter @BethKesh for irreverent snark or go to www.emfaulds. com to find out more about her writing.

Requiem Played on a Decastring

Jack Schouten

Today I am a woman.

I sit up on a gurney. The gurney protrudes from a white wall. There is an identical gurney beside me, upon which lies a body. The room is empty but for the two gurneys, a door, and a mirror.

Yesterday's body is completely still. I swing my legs over the gurney, dismount, and approach him. I gently prod the synthetic flesh of his cheek, then do the same to my own. No difference. I press a button on the wall and my old body retracts into it. It will make its way through the arcane tunnels of the Manufactory to be deconstructed and recycled. I feel a fleeting sense of sadness, of loss.

I sit opposite the mirror. I flex. I stretch my arms, arch my back. The last woman I was had been heavier. This time I am lithe, athletic. There is muscle on my stomach; my breasts are smaller; my legs are longer, shaped by exercise that never took place. I have fiery red hair in a short ponytail. My eyes are green. My skin is pale, with the subtlest of tan lines. My nails are

Art: Andrew Owens

painted a sheening viridian. A tattoo: black geometric lines and red spatters, begins under my left armpit and extends to my right hip. I like it. My pubic hair is styled neat and narrow. I bear the scar of a fictional appendectomy.

I am heterosexual.

I am a walking cover story.

The man I was yesterday had a slight paunch and an aching knee (a sport-related ACL rupture), giving my gait a sway and a limp; movement in this body is effortless and fluid.

I head to the locker room. The locker bears my ident, scans my newly-formed retina, and opens. The clothes I find inside are comfortable, practical but inviting. They reveal sections of my tattoo.

.Forum interrupts my thoughts:

– *Greetings, Essa.*

I like that name.

– *I am downloading the datapack for your objective now. As always, the very best of luck, and long live the Collective.*

When I repeat these last words aloud, my voice is…mellifluous. I like this body a lot.

I leave for the city outside.

The city thrums. I find myself in an entertainment district – the distant war has not blunted the sharpness of people's desire to get off their heads. Adverts blink into existence over facades of drug bars and pool houses; street vendors screech; electric dancers twirl for credits and applause.

In this maze of deafening nightclubs, he frequents quieter places; he is good with his money. He likes to gamble, though he is not an addict. He prefers conversation at a low level, not yelling into ears over thumping hexcore tunes. He enjoys orchestras. He is a fair player of several instruments, though not confident enough to perform in public.

I find, with some surprise, that I know how to play a decastring. These things I learn about myself are affectations, prompts with which to start a conversation. Manipulation is a fine art, and .Forum is a master craftsman.

I meet him in a casino. People play *Virus!* at screens and Rend at tables. A mechanical *maître d'* flits about the place ferrying drinks. Drug bowls bleed psychotropic steam in myriad colours.

I find him playing Crisis, and join the table. Coloured balls and metal cards roll and flick over the segmented playing surface.

He wins a round.

I catch his eye regularly enough to communicate interest, but timidly enough so as not to seem domineering or eager. His romantic history is varied but predictable. He is attracted to intelligence but not pomposity. He likes fashionable quirks like body-modding but would never have any done himself.

He glances at my tattoo as we play.

I win three rounds of Crisis. Some players leave. He wins a round against a fat gentleman, who storms away from the table.

I let him win the next round. I wonder if he notices that I suddenly took uncharacteristic risks and let him put my pieces in Crisis. I slide the cards I lost over to him, and smile.

He smiles back, unsure; cautious. I sense his heartbeat rise.

The next round, I decimate his pieces ruthlessly. Even the umpire seems impressed.

He blows air out of his cheeks. "Well played," he says. He is tipsy; the *maître d'* is eager to keep him at the table, and plies him with alacrity. "Would you like a drink?"

I say that I would. I say my name is Essa (oh, voids, I really like my name) and he tells me his.

We find a table. I learn that my taste in cocktails is bitter and dry. He likes fruit.

"I'm just an analyst," he tells me. "Decided to do my bit for the war. When they load up the gunships, I check their course and destination, provide a roster for what materiel the troops are going to need. Some of the stuff, you wouldn't believe..."

I ask him why he doesn't go off and fight. I know the answer to this already (not only is he a pacifist, but he is downright terrified of the enemy) but I listen intently, saving his every word to the substrate that constitutes my brain; I may repeat something later, some detail that would show how much I listen, that I care for what he has to say.

"I don't believe in war," he says, with a hint of sanctimony. "I know, call me a hypocrite. Everyone else does – but it's our fault that negotiations with the Xhent broke down."

I say that the Xhent should not have been contacted by the Collective in the first place, that they are so truly alien, so different from the races we already live alongside, so profoundly *otherly* in their culture and etiquette that it was a folly to enter into any kind of deal at all.

"Well, I can't disagree with that," he says, sipping his cocktail. "If you poke a juliprae with a stick, you're going to get eaten. And that's what we fucking did."

I ask him what he means by that.

"The Xhent just see things differently. Disagreeing with them is poking them with that stick. They're ... killing machines, you know? Why enter into a deal with these psychos in the first place? I mean, have you *seen* a Xhent?"

I have. Not in person, but preoccupation with the enemy is so entrenched in the war-time zeitgeist that information on the Xhent is installed in our BIOS, our base operating systems.

I say they have too many teeth.

"Too many fucking *mouths*. If the Collective knew what was best for all concerned, they'd call a ceasefire. We're losing. Miserably."

I say that he is missing the point. The attack on Hunter's Run, the pulse bomb that started the war, *was* an attack on the

Collective, whether Hunter's Run was a devolved administration or not; it's just that most of the Collective have kept their noses out.

"Well," he says, pompously. "Screw the Collective. Like I said: poked them with a stick."

I decide I do not like my target very much. He is a coward.

There is a pause. I sip my cocktail.

"Where were you when the pulse bomb hit?"

I give him the story.

"I was in here, funnily enough," he replies. "We felt it, the city felt it. Drinks quivered, like this." He demonstrates. "News flashes popped up instantly."

I tell a similar tale of the gigadeaths at Hunter's Run.

He goes back to the war; he cannot help it.

"You know, half the reason we're losing the fight is that people are too scared of the augmentations needed to meet the Xhent in combat. You know about those?"

I say I don't.

"They turn you into ... I don't know, pure muscle. Takes days just to learn how to walk again, lugging around all that power. Even heard they're going to bring in conscription. That happens and I'm on the first flitship to Forrenze's Recluse."

He is scared of the modifications. I don't tell him conscription has already begun, has been going on for a while. Or that within a few days he'll be a different man, off on a starship to fight the rending mandibles of the Xhent. Or that, in a way, this is an interview, which he will pass whether he likes it or not.

"Don't get me wrong. I'm not a conspiracy theorist. All that shit about androids that force you into the augmentations without you knowing? Nah." He laughs. I laugh too.

"I love your tattoo," he says. "Did it hurt?"

I invent a story of patience and pain in a tattoo parlour that doesn't exist. Now is the right time; his heart is racing, but he feels in control, drunk enough to be confident but polite enough to wait for me to move. I show a little more of the tattoo, trace its path over my clothes, just a little suggestively.

He shifts in his seat, nonchalantly takes a sip of his cocktail. He is struggling with the beginnings of arousal.

I lean over and kiss him.

I ask if he would like to see all of the tattoo.

His apartment is a short flexride from the city, in Hour's Mount. It is modest, and tastefully furnished. A glowplace in the centre of the main room drapes the apartment in a blue light. He changes it to red shortly after we enter. The city sprawls herself along the horizon beyond the wall-to-wall window.

Instruments hang from walls. A decastring is propped up against a soft violet sofa.

He heads to the kitchen to pour us drinks. When he returns with two large glasses of hetchwine I am naked, and playing the decastring on the sofa. He is agog.

I have not been given the knowledge of music before. The way my fingers flick across its strings, the technique of shifting a palm slightly to deaden the sound for effect, the resulting vibration across the hand; the glissandos, the trills; the chords dripping with feeling; the sheer *perfectness* of it, brings up an emotion I don't remember ever feeling. It is an upwelling, as if the biotech in my substrates is suddenly operating at double time. For a moment it is just me and the music in a vacuum of bliss. Everything disappears. The war. The target. My directive. Everything but these ten strings gently plucked, their wondrous music, and me and my fingers, effervesces from existence. I will never hear a sound more beautiful than this, whose name I do not even know.

The piece ends, and with surprise I realise I have shed a tear, and wonder why the factories even gave me that affectation. I quietly scan the datapack and find, with some disappointment, that he likes women who show emotion, as if he is attracted to the vulnerability he believes he lacks, and subconsciously seeks it out in others. The tear is automatic, a manipulation of melancholy. I feel anger for a moment.

I apologise and invent a story about my mother playing the same piece for me as a child.

"Don't be sorry, Essa..." (my substrates quiver at the sound of my name) "...that was beautiful. *Venthor's Requiem.* Fabulously difficult to play. And you played it perfectly. When did you learn? Here." He hands me the glass of hetchwine as I replace the decastring on the sofa.

Venthor's Requiem. I make a note never to forget it.

For a moment he seemed so entranced by my playing that he forgot I was naked. I sit confidently, my legs together, my back straight. He traces the lines of my tattoo with a finger. I conjure goosebumps for him. We each down our drinks, and I take him to the bedroom.

He doesn't even wonder how I already knew where it is.

As a lover he is gentle, but unconvincing in his gentleness. He makes love with a sort of reluctance, a lack of conviction. Like him, it is pleasant but ultimately disappointing.

That will change, I wager, in the unlikely event he ever fucks again.

His movements and rhythm are somehow disingenuous, as if he is acting as a selfless lover who cannot hide the fact that this pleasure is for him and him alone. He strokes my tattoo as we move together, and gradually his pace quickens, and quickens, and he can hide his selfishness no longer. I thank .Forum that it gives us the ability to feel pleasure. Though, I wonder if their pleasure is somehow different from ours, that there are feelings I will never feel no matter how well-designed our substrates and synapses are.

As he finishes, I think of *Venthor's Requiem,* and silently thank him; he is not the only one who has received a gift before he goes off to war.

I transmit the gene-program while he is still inside me. Like always, I feel a kind of turning in my stomach. It is not entirely unpleasureable.

As is standard, I spend the night. Half asleep, he muses about one day finding love.

When he wakes up, he complains of feeling unwell. He goes to the bathroom, grunting with pain. I quietly walk to the main room and get dressed. I sit down and play the decastring with distracted nonchalance as his moans of pain become guttural. Over the music, I hear him vomit.

"Essa!" Even in anger my name sounds beautiful.

He comes into the room. I stop playing. He is pale and sweating. His muscles quiver; already the gene-program is building new muscle, increasing bone density. His reflexes and senses will change soon.

I tell him not to be alarmed, that this is normal.

"Normal? *Normal?*" he screams. He stalks towards me, bent over, his shaking hands kneading his stomach. "What did you *do?* What have you *done to me?*"

I ask him to be calm. I apologise. He takes the decastring and hurls it against the wall. It explodes into pieces. Its strings break and twang horribly. I feel sadness.

The aggression components are already working on him. He will be a good soldier.

He turns from the ruined instrument. "You *bitch*, what have you done?"

I let him punch me three times before incapacitating him. I twist his arm on his fourth strike and with my other arm I chop at the nerve between shoulder and neck. He crumples, wailing.

His skin ripples. His screams of pain increase in intensity. He will not be moving from the floor for a few hours yet. I walk over to the smashed decastring, rend a piece in half, and put the little chunk of wood in my pocket.

I apologise again as I leave, though I'm not sure if it is to the decastring or the groaning, crumpled man becoming a killing machine on the floor of his apartment. .Forum will be watching, I tell him, in case anything goes wrong.

He screams after me as I close the door.

I awake on a gurney.

I sit up and look at myself in the mirror. I am about sixty years of age. Hair once black, now salt-and-pepper, slicked back; a pair of eyes whose wrinkles betray many years of laughter. I'm not in great shape. Little rolls of fat crease my belly, but she will forget about that, and concentrate on my smile and infectious laugh instead; the target is not a shallow woman.

I am a widower. I will be bewitched by her.

Essa lies on the gurney next to me, motionless, her eyes now silver-in-silver, washed out, the life literally gone from them.

"Goodbye, Essa," I say, and press the button. She disappears into the bowels of the Manufactory.

I find a piece of wood on the shelf in my locker, alongside other little trinkets and trophies. .Forum does not publicly allow this, but I suspect it turns a blind camera to my habit.

I dress. I walk through the halls of .Forum, humming *Venthor's Requiem*, and suddenly find the piece slightly annoying, shrill; a little gauche. An earworm I cannot shake. I shut it out, and eventually forget it.

I walk into the city a man.

Jack Schouten's science fiction has been published in *Jupiter* (Anthilion's Eyes), *Shoreline of Infinity* ("Neme"), and *Clarkesworld Magazine* ("Sephine and the Leviathan", featured in Baen Books' Best SF of the Year 2016).
He owns a dog, a cat, and a tenant, who is also a cat. He lives and works in Surrey.

The Librarian

Adriana Kantcheva

The August sky was spilling its insides in unbroken rods of water. By the time I reached the library at Trinity College in Dublin, my dress was completely soaked. I wondered if they would allow me in so wet: yet another wretched tourist.

A shadow moved beside the library. The rain stopped whipping in my face for a second and the shadow resolved into an old man wrapped in a rain poncho. Strands of wet hair crawled from underneath his hood, which couldn't keep his long, sharp nose dry. A curving forefinger emerged from underneath the poncho and beckoned to me.

Curiosity gnawed at my caution. I lived my life inside the books I read, wondering when my story would begin. This seemed to be it. I hurried towards the old man. I was about to reach him when he disappeared into a gap. It bore a street sign: Old Library Lane.

I peeked in. The old man skulked down the rain-sodden passage. He opened a door and disappeared into the library building, leaving the door ajar. A wizened hand appeared through the crack and again beckoned to me.

I hesitated. But I so wished to participate in a story worth telling. I pulled the door open to reveal lantern-lit stairs spiralling down. The man's poncho disappeared behind the nearest turn.

"Where are we going?" I asked when I caught up with my guide.

"To the library."

"I thought the library was above us."

"Not all of it."

I ignored a shiver. "Who are you?"

"The Librarian."

He smiled a graveyard of browned teeth and removed his dripping poncho to uncover a weathered suit at least two sizes too large. The tails of the bleached coat hung below the backs of his knees.

"Doesn't the university employ several librarians?"

"But I am the Librarian." He stopped. "Here we are."

We halted in front of a second door. I raised an eyebrow at the inscription above it: Caution! Live stories.

We entered a large chamber. Candle flames danced on massive chandeliers. Cabinets reached up to the ceiling, forming a labyrinth of aisles. And the books? There were thousands and thousands of them! Some with ragged edges, others bound in shiny new leather. Some contained not but ten pages, others could stop doors, but all were breathing, whispering with a dry susurrus as if pages turned, covers flapped.

"Let's see," the Librarian said. He looked me over. "Definitely a hardcover. Title in uneven letters, I think. Paper of medium weight."

As he talked, his hands wove colourful jets in the stagnant air. The room spun about me.

"Eleven-point font size, I'd say." His voice was growing dim. "Gothic style. Page numbering in the bottom margin, cantered. Definitely cantered..."

The Librarian was still talking, but I could hardly make out the words. He picked me up.

"Bookcase 85 is the right place for you," I barely heard him say.

Adriana Kantcheva is a Bulgarian writer of speculative fiction who lives in southern Germany with her family. She has a Ph.D. in molecular biology and has worked as a science editor.
Find more about Adriana at https://catchingwords.com/ or get in touch with her on Twitter (@AKantcheva) or Instagram (adriana.kantcheva).

City of Corporate-Sanctioned Delights

B.G. Alder

When Brick and I staggered out of the atmo-entry taxi, my nostrils filled with the many odors of BLAM!™, City of Corporate-Sanctioned Delights. Fry grease and exhaust stink hovered over the crush of bodies. But I'd just spent eight consecutive weeks at the station, combing through algorithm-generated jokes and breathing my co-workers' recycled farts. I gulped down the fetid air of the docks like that shit was ambrosia.

Art: Skylar Kardon

BLAM!™ caters to people like Brick and me, working stiffs who get four days of shore leave at a time. While it's possible to go drink matcha lattes at a tidy Korean-style café, the dominant aesthetic is neon. They flash strobe lights in our faces until we keel over, stunned like city pigeons. Then they go through our pockets. Wherever we wake up, they tell us we got our money's worth.

As we plunged into the milling crowds, Brick was already looking wrecked. Their hair appeared electrocuted. Their pink crop top was stained with something I hoped was coffee. You'd dumped them over V-chat the night before.

"Hey," Brick shouted. The thump of bass was vibrating down to the roots of our teeth. "At least my big messy break-up came *before* shore leave."

I nodded, sweating. Obviously, this was not a good place to process one's feelings. But reading algorithm-generated sitcom gags all day will poison the brain. If the algorithm were writing this little outing to BLAM!™, Brick and I would get wasted on fruity cocktails, steal a parade float, crash it into a wall, fuck amidst the wreckage, and then get bailed out of jail by some repentant version of you, Brick's gorgeous ex. The conditioning had gone so far that a little goblin part of me actually wanted to do this, although Brick and I are good friends, and not each other's types.

Brick was already walking into a bar (there's a joke lurking there, but I'll leave it to the computers). Fake palm trees. Teal pools of vodka Jell-o, festooned with candy sharks. I watched Brick buy two very tall alcoholic slushies the color of spam and take them to go.

"I know you don't want to hear this," I said, as we elbowed our way down the boulevard, "but I don't think you should get wasted right now."

Brick took a long, noisy slurp from their drink.

"Brick, you said you loved her."

"Yeah, but what else am I going to do for four days?"

I didn't interpret this as a rhetorical question. We needed a distraction, an unsanctioned delight. But our seventy-hour work week had atrophied my creative and literal muscles. Brick and I are not inventors. We pick the rhinestones out of the shit.

"Let's do something the algorithm would never come up with," I said, aware of how lame this would sound.

To my surprise, Brick perked up.

"No alcoholic hijinks," I ruled. "No funky costumes. Minimal interpersonal drama. A weekend completely unfit for streaming."

"Okay," Brick said, with a glassy-eyed stare. "Let's go touch a cow."

"That sounds amazing," I said, mustering a ghastly grin. "Very tactile, very wacky. Definitely what I would like to be doing right now."

"Are you being sarcastic?"

I ignored them and started typing on my phone. Whatever happened, it was better than watching Brick slam down tequila shots with strangers. 'Cows blam (tm) where' generated a few commonly asked questions: 'What continent do cows come from? Are cows man made? Where can I tip cows?' More promisingly, I found a link to the only cow café in the city. I showed Brick the logo, a smiling cow offering up her own milk in a pitcher.

"Oh hell nah," Brick said. "I'm not drinking that bitch's juice. Look at her eyes."

Her eyes were, indeed, disconcertingly blank. But when I pulled up a digital map to the cow café and started walking, Brick followed me without question.

"Counter or booth?" the hostess asked, when we bumbled in, expecting – what, exactly, I wonder?

The café didn't smell of manure, or even warm hay. An espresso machine squealed. Buttery coffee smells wafted through the air. All the wait staff in sight wore head-to-toe cow suits, replete with pink silicone udders and polyester fur.

"Nope," Brick said, spinning on their heel.

I grabbed Brick's arm and hauled them back from the exit. Unlike most of the waiters, with their bovine fur-helmets, the hostess' primate face was visible under a fuzzy, black-and-white hood.

"Excuse me, citizen," I said, in my most adult voice. "Are you familiar with the award-winning, long-running situational comedy, 'Stuck in a Time Warp With You'?"

She licked her chapped lips and shot me a hard glance. Somewhere behind the mascara, I thought I saw a grudging glint of recognition.

"We are valued staff writers, here to conduct some research for a super-secret future story arc." I glanced at Brick, hoping for back-up, but they were busy stealing fistfuls of complimentary mints from an unguarded bowl. "Do you have, perhaps, a very small, non-human cow available for us to pet?"

With a single limp gesture, the hostess presented the costumed herd, the wall art above the red pleather booths, and the surprisingly banal-looking patrons. "We have many cows."

"Looks like a great place, but a little niche for our purposes." Out of the corner of my eye, I glimpsed a waiter squeezing synthetic half 'n' half out of his fake rubbery tit, straight into somebody's coffee cup. "What's this milk made of, anyway?"

She shrugged. "Lab-grown yeasts."

"Do you know where we can buy the real thing?"

The hostess' penciled-in eyebrows shot up. "You want to drink something that came out of a bio cow? Like, one that shits on the ground?"

"So what if we do?" Brick interjected, in a tone that worried me right away. They were crunching down free peppermints, not using their inside voice. "We want to feel something that isn't derived from petroleum. Eat something that isn't made from a chemical soup. We're tired of bull shit. The metaphorical kind."

Having made this speech, Brick met my gaze once and then looked away, plunging into moody silence.

"Ohh-kay," said the hostess, not quite rolling her eyes. "There is a high-end organic creamery on the edge of town. It's pricey, and you'll have to take the train. But I think they keep a few shitbeasts."

"Beautiful," I said, noting down the name.

A tablet glowed between the hostess' hands. When I gave it a tap with my phone, transferring a tip, it emitted a low, unmistakable moo.

Of course, there are a few public transit routes that can get you out of BLAM!™. But the city fathers made sure that trying to escape the municipal limits would be even more unpleasant and exhausting than staying put. After a bad, long wander, Brick and I found one of several obscure stops for the Green Line, a rickety train on stilts that is best known for having once unexpectedly caught fire.

The Green Train is forever flying the same route above the city, screeching and circling like a one-winged bird. When we rounded the top of the colossal staircase, the last passenger car was just rattling out of sight. We settled down to wait. In place of club music, distant taxi horns blared. Shreds of plastic bag blew and scuttled between the benches. If we'd still had trees, and seasons, they could've been autumn leaves.

We'd barely spoken since the cow café. Brick didn't seem tipsy anymore, just distant, watching pigeons with missing toes peck at crumbs around our feet.

"Do you really feel that way?" I asked. "About bull shit? Because it is our livelihood."

Brick peered up at the overcast sky. I followed their gaze, trying to see what they saw. Pollution, sure. But it was good to look at something other than ceiling – a clutter of brownish clouds, shifting with wind and heat.

"I was twenty-two years old before I learned that pineapples are real and blue raspberries are not," Brick said. "Some days I just want to knit, slowly. Get rained on. Put my hands in some dirt."

Ever since arriving fresh-faced at the orbital station of an entertainment giant to join a 'high-intensity work culture' and 'make the galaxy laugh,' Brick and I had bunked together. We'd eaten side-by-side in the mess every day. Although we'd seen each other's worst drafts, and bare butts, we seldom touched. I put a hand on their shoulder, feeling like a creep.

"Does this have anything to do with Selena?"

"It's the long-distance thing." Brick's eyes were wet, although mostly they sounded angry. "I have to stay on a company rig. It's in the fucking contract. They charge me for my room, they charge me for my meals, they charge for transportation. Three years and somehow I'm still in the red?"

Some social scientist must have observed the optimal time range for platonic touch, but I hadn't thought to comb through the research. Now I removed my hand from Brick's upper arm, worried I'd done it wrong.

"I'll never start a farm," Brick said, burying their head in their hands. "I'll never even have a container garden. What's the point?"

Our job may be degrading, but there is a kind of glamor to it. We live in space. We write TV. The algorithm does most of the work for our show and all the others; there aren't many human artists left anymore. But the chaos of mammalian humor eludes the usual formulas, enough to justify a few fleshy assistants. Brick and I had clawed our way into two of those slots, through means and methods I blush to recount. And we'd been paying for the privilege ever since.

I should admit that, unlike Brick, I wasn't wallowing in debt. My parents still wired me credits on birthdays and New Year's. Brick and I never talked about this difference between us. But then, I thought I knew how bad it was.

The Green Train came at last, bound for the outer districts. We found two hard-backed seats among the day-shift workers.

Around us, people in scrubs, sequins, and coveralls popped in their earbuds and let their faces go slack. Below the tracks, the blazing city slid by, shrieking for our attention. But I was looking at the deserted platforms, the weedy hell strips. Vines were snaking their way up through the cracks.

By the time the Green Train clattered to a halt, we weren't in BLAM!™ anymore. The commuters scattered, heads down. The air had gone blue and cool against my skin. I flapped my arms a few times, just feeling the breeze. There isn't night where I'm from – only a few hours when the sky goes pinkish gray.

Usually I navigated for us both. But Brick had already pulled out their phone and turned a corner. I stood at the mouth of the empty street, watching them go. Aside from the clean white glow of their phone, the place was dingy, scribbled with tags. Metal lattices shielded the windows. The shops and stalls were shuttered with corrugated steel. Up ahead, I even spotted an alley. They had alleys here, for God's sake.

"Wait," I hissed, my chest getting tight.

I wanted to warn Brick about muggers, and diseases, and logistical constraints. This seemed an unlikely place for a dairy. Even if it were here, it would be closed when we arrived. Soon the Green Line would stop running, and where the hell would we sleep?

But Brick was already disappearing into the dark. I sprinted after them, faster than I'd run in my whole noodly life. When I caught up, my heart pounding, Brick didn't even look up from their phone. On the screen, greasy with fingerprints, a blinking dot (us) was approaching a star.

The clustered buildings opened up into a long, wide, industrial street lined with warehouses. In the gaps between fluorescent lamps where the light began to dim, my adrenaline spiked. I imagined the sound of tailing footsteps. Then we came to the next lamp, and the brightness dulled my senses again.

Even here, the silence wasn't complete. I heard a high, electric hum; the distant roar of atmo-entry. My cheap jelly loafers blistered my toes. The last time I walked so far in one stretch, I'd been living planet-side in my parents' gated compound, where the fake lawns unfurled for empty acres and got shat on by tiny dogs.

"It's supposed to be here," Brick said at last, staring at a stretch of colossal unmarked fence.

I followed their gaze up, and up, and up. It looked like a border wall, spikes and barbs gleaming from its unfriendly top.

"It'll be electrified," I said. "They'll have cameras, and alarms—"

Brick put a finger to their lips. I listened, expecting the tread of a rent-a-cop, come to drag us back to wherever we were supposed to be. Instead, I heard a sound, starting low and rising into a reed-instrument moan. Another voice rumbled in answer, deeper and more insistent than the last. Unseen creatures shuffled and snorted in the dark. My synapses fired at random, trying to link the grunts and calls with something I could understand: circus elephants. Brachiosaurus herd. Bellowing humans. Whoever these guys were, they were tripping balls.

Something warm and damp brushed my hand. For an instant, I was paralyzed, wondering if I'd been licked. But it was only Brick reaching for me. We clutched each other and faced the forms looming out of the dusk. If it hadn't been for Brick's hand in mine, I would've turned tail. But Brick held me steady. Soon I couldn't look away.

The beasts trotting toward us were too huge, too rectangular, too quick to be cows. With them came a gust of warm, musky smell, not a sewage stink like I'd been led to believe. Strangest of all, every inch of them was in motion – round ears flicking, hairy tails swishing. Even their skins twitched. They crowded the other side of the gate and showed us their enormous white teeth, groaning and shouting, like we were supposed to understand.

There was no question – they'd made a bee line for Brick and me. And now, they were trying to tell us something. Their eyes were round and dark, fringed in thick lashes like a cartoon girl's.

"Are these cows?" whispered Brick.

"They must be genetic mods," I said, with a conviction I didn't feel. "Who the fuck would try to milk a thing like that?"

Whatever they were, they were still yelling. I glanced over my shoulder, dancing from one sore foot to the other. With all this noise, an authority was bound to find us. I didn't know which rule we were breaking, but I was convinced we'd done something wrong.

"They are," Brick was saying, with tears in their eyes. "They *are* cows. I love them. And look – they love me."

Before I could stop them, Brick thrust a hand between the thick metal bars of the gate. I watched, seized with envy and horror, as a thick primordial tongue emerged from one animal's mouth. In a single deft swipe, it slimed the salty knuckles of Brick's outstretched hand.

I am not proud to say this: I screamed. Brick screamed. In the shadows of the creamery, a gruff voice shouted, "Hey!"

Whoever it was, we did not stick around to find out. With their unslobbered hand, Brick was still holding mine. When they ran, I ran. My useless shoes tripped me. So I kicked them off. My soft, blistered soles slapped against the stinging asphalt. Pebbles and grit dug into my skin. But for the first time in my life, I felt fast, almost strong.

Beside me, Brick was gasping for breath. When we couldn't run anymore, we doubled over and wheezed. Nobody was after us. We heard no brachiosaurs over the buzz of the lights. When we finally looked up, we were laughing.

"The cow touched you," I said.

Every shore leave must come to an end. But this one, at least, we were going to remember. On the dawn of day four, Brick and I stepped into line with our co-workers, looking smug, well-rested, and bright-eyed. We'd spent the last two days of our freedom reconstructing our adventure in a 420-friendly hostel and watching archival footage of farms. For once, I wasn't concerned that Brick would throw up in the scanning chamber.

You don't need to be sober to pass an orbital re-entry check. You don't even technically need to be conscious. But when I stepped out of the sliding glass door, my body scan blinking red, a security officer pulled me aside. Brick was already waiting. They looked at me and shrugged.

A supervisor was called. When she arrived, she sat us down and cut to the chase. "Where did you go?"

"Nowhere, really," Brick said.

"Do you have any idea where you might've picked up a biological contaminant?"

"Nope."

The supervisor took us in with a long, slow blink. "You don't have any communicable disease, as far as we know. But there are traces of foreign matter that I can't classify. It's in your feet," she said, looking at me. "And on your pants," she said, to Brick.

I glanced sidelong at Brick. They mimed wiping off a spitty hand on their cargo shorts.

"I've ordered a fourteen-day quarantine before you enter the station," the supervisor told us briskly. "We're just playing it safe."

"That's great and all," said Brick, who'd actually read our contracts, "but we can't. We only had four days off, and we've used them."

"What about sick leave?"

"We're writers, man. You think we get benefits?"

The supervisor frowned, and held up a finger. "Let me make a quick call."

Several hours and one bureaucratic odyssey later, Brick and I found ourselves booted onto the street. More grateful writers with better hygiene would soon be imported from the surface. Our clothes and incidentals – one box each – would soon be rocketed down. As the last of our former colleagues boarded company taxis, we sat on the curb in high-UV sunshine, staring down the barrel of our new, untethered lives.

You don't know me, Selena, so I hope you'll forgive me for sending you this account. In a few days, I'll head home to the mansion basement, the disappointed parents, the novel no one will ever read. I will walk the tiny dog and sleep until noon. Brick is welcome there, on the downstairs couch. But the green grass is just baked sheets of astro-turf. You can't find dirt there. You can't even find rain.

I think you called Brick from your balcony once. You laughed at all their jokes, and sat in your own slice of warm, moving air. If you want to plant something there in the light, don't reply to this message. Write to Brick. And do it soon.

B.G. Alder (she/they) is a genderqueer, Seattle-based writer spoon-fed on Jewish folklore and Star Trek. A University of Montana MFA graduate, and Fulbright Creative Writing grantee, her work has appeared in *Jewish Quarterly*, *StoryQuarterly*, and the *Santa Fe Writers Project Quarterly*, and received the Amy Levy Short Story Prize.

THE LIVING MUSEUM

Tim Major

E d straightened his bowler before continuing his stroll
alongside the tram lines. He swung his briefcase, enjoying
the warmth of the sun on his face, but then told himself
to behave soberly, more in character. As he passed one of the
iron lampposts he perceived a glimmer from the lens behind its
thick glass, suggesting that someone in head office was already
watching. He checked his fob watch: fifteen minutes to ten. The
main entrance wouldn't yet be open, but the queues would be
growing at the ticket office. A tram passed him in the opposite
direction. When it returned it would be filled with visitors.

Smoke already plumed from the houses in the village. He
would have to have a word with somebody. The fires needn't be
lit until the visitors were actually within the museum grounds.
Coal was more expensive than people realised, and the museum

97

prided itself on authenticity whenever possible. Dry ice and a chemical scent produced in a lab just wouldn't do.

He was surprised by a noise to his left as he passed through the village. Ann Wheeler stood in the doorway of the schoolhouse, beckoning to two children still in the playground rolling their metal hoops. As they ducked either side of her to slip into the building, she looked up.

"Morning, Mr Piggot," she said cheerfully.

Ed craned his neck. "Are those your children, Ann?"

"Of course, sir."

"I didn't know you had a family."

"Oh. No, sir." Her cheeks flushed. "Not my own, in that sense."

"Are they ill?"

"No, sir. Do they look so, to you?"

"Not at all. Look, you don't need to call me 'sir' while nobody's looking, okay? But clearly those children aren't visitors, because the visitors haven't been let in yet. And it's term time. So why aren't they at school?"

Ann turned to look into the schoolhouse, then faced him again. "Are you quite well yourself, Mr Piggot?"

"It's out of hours, so I'm just Ed. Look, I haven't got time for this. But those kids need registering as temp workers. So please tell whoever brought them here to get onto it."

Ann nodded slowly without any suggestion of comprehension. Ed puffed his cheeks and hurried on his way. He wouldn't allow himself to be held up from his final checks before the start of the day. He checked his fob watch again and, for the first time, wondered whether it, too, contained a camera.

At the window of the classroom he stopped again, bemused. The room was full of children. Fifteen of them or more, all sitting at their desks. He saw Ann enter. When she called out, "Good morning children," the children all chanted, "Good morning, Mrs Trembath," without prompting. Ed shielded his eyes to block out the sunlight. All of the children were in period dress, and convincingly shabby outfits at that. They couldn't *all* be temp workers; it must be a school trip – but then where was the teacher that had accompanied them to the living museum? Either way, school visits were supposed to be restricted to the same hours as ordinary visitors. Ed would have to take it up with management.

The short walk to the high street was pleasant enough to clear his mind of any lingering annoyance. He whistled as he walked. He counted three horses in the field to his right, whereas there ought to be four – he would have to ask someone about that, though it was less urgent than the shop checks, as coach rides were only available after lunchtime in order to give visitors the chance to wander around a little first. To his left the exhibition space was just grass and dust. He smiled at the thought that in only a few weeks, yellow-jacketed contractors would arrive to set up the Victorian fairground, including the ever-popular Gallopers, and the temporary skating rink, and all of the shrubs would be coated with fake snow. This year Ed would pay particular attention to ensuring that the generator that produced the snow and ice was well hidden behind the coconut shy sideshow. Anything that undermined the illusion was totally unacceptable.

He arrived at the high street later than intended, so he would have to complete his final checks quickly. He hurried past the bandstand and up the steps to the tearoom. He squinted into the dim interior.

"Hey!" he called out. "Is anyone here?"

Rachael emerged from the back room, wiping her hands on her apron, which was covered in flour – a nice touch, given that all the sandwiches and loaves arrived by truck each morning rather than being baked on site. It occurred to Ed that he hadn't seen the truck arrive this morning.

"You'd better get the lights on," Ed said, already turning to leave. "The first tram load will be here soon."

Rachael hesitated, then nodded and went to the first of the wall lamps. She tutted as she fiddled with the small knob, then it lit with a *whoomph*.

"Electrics on the blink?" Ed said.

"I can't afford such things as electric lights, sir," Rachael replied.

Ed rolled his eyes. He scanned the wooden counter. "Where's the machine? Everybody wants contactless payments these days."

"Sir?"

"Contactless, Rachael."

She took a step back, holding up her hands as if she had been apprehended by police. "Sorry, sir."

Ed let out a sigh of exasperation. Why was everybody being so uncooperative this morning? He glanced at the black reflective surface behind the counter, upon which was stencilled the name of the tearoom and line drawings of cups and saucers. Either there were cameras installed behind the surface, relaying a constant feed to head office, or it was a two-way mirror, or both. Perhaps one of the senior managers was standing behind it at this moment, tutting at the state of things.

"Just get yourself up to speed, please," he said to Rachael, already hurrying away. "Be a bit professional."

In the stables he found Freddy sitting on a stool, holding a horse's leg gently, peering at the underside of its hoof.

Ed nodded approvingly. "Lovely. They'll enjoy seeing this."

"Who's that, sir?" Freddy replied, looking up. His face was streaked with muck, rather more of it than seemed plausible.

Ed gestured in the direction from which he had come. "*Them.* Who do you think?"

"Shouldn't you be at work yourself, Mr Piggot?"

"What do you think I'm doing right now?"

Freddy peered up at the bright blue sky. "Perhaps taking the air?"

"I'm checking everybody's ready for the day, as usual. I'm doing exactly what's written in my job description." Ed's eyes darted. He didn't know where the cameras were installed in the stables.

"But you're a solicitor, sir."

Ed looked down at his suit. "They had to outfit me as *something*. What do you expect me to do – sit in an office in the hope that imaginary clients might come along? That's not much of a spectacle for the crowds, is it?"

The horse shuffled. Freddy grimaced as he popped a stone from its hoof, then he released the animal's leg.

"I'm sorry, Mr Piggot. You're running rings around me. I just thought you were a busy man, that's all."

Ed couldn't see any cameras or any reflective surfaces. In a low voice he hissed, "And I am. I'm your supervisor, for crying out loud. But I'm trained in events management, not the law. I wouldn't know where to start as a solicitor." He popped open his briefcase to show that it was empty.

Freddy rubbed his jaw in a display of confusion.

The horse whinnied. Ed backed away. "Are you going to put the stone back in its hoof?"

"Why would I do that?"

"So you can remove it again when the visitors arrive."

Freddy just stared.

Ed clenched his fists. "You're slowing me down. I have to get on."

He didn't stop to talk in the sweet shop or the chemist's, and he only put his head into the doorway of the printers long enough to confirm that he could hear the presses thudding away upstairs.

Pam, who played the part of Miss Florence Smith the music teacher, shrieked as he strode into her house.

"You can't just walk in here!" she snapped. She was standing at the rear door of her kitchen, a bucket of water in hand, on the verge of tossing its contents into the yard.

"I didn't hear music from outside, so I came in to tell you that you need to get cracking."

"What in the Lord's name are you talking about?"

Ed rubbed the bridge of his nose. He tried to ignore the lamps and framed pictures, any of which might hide a camera. "Play the piano, Pam. It's your job."

"My job is *teaching* the piano, Mr Piggot. It'd do nobody any good if I spent my free minutes playing it and ignoring my housekeeping. You'd best look to your own duties rather than deliver sermons to others."

"Pam—"

She raised an eyebrow. "Miss Florence Smith."

"If you insist."

"I do insist. Furthermore, I insist that you don't go strolling into women's homes without a care. Get out, Mr Piggot. Make a nuisance of yourself elsewhere."

She approached him, brandishing the bucket. As Ed backed out of the house, he conceded to himself that visitors, especially kids, would probably be thrilled by her performance. Perhaps mixing up the routine wasn't such a bad thing.

Outside, he checked his watch again and gazed along the road. A bus pulled into its stop. To his surprise, the few passengers that alighted were staff, judging by appearances – a couple of men in suits as smart as his own, and women wearing dresses and bonnets. Ed didn't recognise them. The street was beginning to fill up, and yet there were still no visitors, nobody in modern dress.

He stumbled on the pavement before he entered the Co-op department store, which he had been told had been reconstructed after being brought to the living museum, brick by brick, from Annfield Plain in County Durham.

"Are you unwell?" Daniel said from behind the counter, peering through his half-moon glasses.

"A little lightheaded, that's all. Do you have something I could munch on?"

Daniel's eyes flicked to the produce contained in the tall shelves that surrounded him. "Well, yes, of course."

"I mean real food, not set dressing. Some of those broken biscuits that the kids like. I've only got fifty pence, though. Will that do?"

Daniel chuckled, but stopped when he registered Ed's confusion. "A ha'penny will be just fine, Mr Piggot."

Ed patted his pockets but couldn't find his cash. He must have left it in his jeans, which were still in the staff changing rooms behind the ticket office.

Daniel handed him a paper bag filled with broken biscuits. "You'd better take it all the same. And perhaps you'd do best to consult with Mr Coulson at the chemist's too, Mr Piggot."

Ed crammed biscuits into his mouth. "I'm getting pretty tired of everybody insisting on remaining in character. I mean, nobody's even arrived yet!" He nodded in the direction of the street, where costumed men and women strolled back and forth. But then, with a flushed sense of contradicting himself, he stared up at the convex mirror in the corner of the dark room. He was being watched. The visitors were only the half of it. Perhaps this delay in their arrival was a test.

Before getting this job at the living museum he had been a team leader at a call centre. Despite the trials of his current role, he didn't think he could bear to return to that sort of work, trapped in a stuffy office all day. But back then he had told himself it was the constant scrutiny that he wanted to escape.

With a start, he realised he was unable to summon an image of his former manager, or even the workplace itself, in his mind's eye. He needed to rest.

"You know what?" he said, almost relishing his increasing lightheadedness, "I swear I'm going to insist my name's changed. I don't know how I ended up saddled with Piggot."

"You're not making a great deal of sense, Mr Piggot," Daniel said, his tone hardening. "Perhaps you ought to return home and allow your wife to see to you."

"My name is Ed Duncan!" Ed shouted in frustration. "And I don't have a wife. Not out there in the real world, and even here in this jumped-up pantomime she's only a name – nobody's even been cast in the role, despite me bringing it up at my last appraisal." He took Daniel's arm, led him to the doorway of the shop, and pointed across the road at the solicitor's house. "There's nobody in that building and it's not even furnished. It's just a façade. The door's painted shut, for God's sake!"

Several people had stopped to watch him. His cheeks flushed at the shame of his unprofessional manner. He felt certain that upper management were watching. Every lamp and every shop window glinted, as did the eyes of the extras playing the pedestrians.

"I'm sorry," he said, patting Daniel's arm and gently pushing him back into the department store. "I'll get a grip on myself. I've got another appraisal coming up, that's all. I'm a bit on edge, focused on visitor appreciation targets, all that sort of thing."

Daniel watched him with a steady gaze. Ed tried to ignore the glimmering in his eyes.

He cleared his throat, loosened and then retied his tie, then turned back to the street, which was now bustling with actors. He checked his fob watch, smiled at it reassuringly in case there really was a camera there, then turned his attention to the corner of the street, where the first tram filled with visitors would surely soon appear.

Tim Major is a writer and freelance editor from York. His books include *Hope Island*, *Snakeskins*, *Universal Language* and a story collection, *And the House Lights Dim*. His short stories have been selected for Best of British Science Fiction and Best Horror of the Year. cosycatastrophes.com

Transmission

Know this:
they are neither more nor less than
       they ever were.

They are the same.
We've not affected them.
We merely translate their brainwaves
       into language
that you can comprehend.

It is your perception that's changed.

So, it was against your will?
Against the will of the populace.
Mea culpa, mea culpa
       mea bloody culpa in spades
          madafaka.
But look at what we have done.

We've cracked open minds.

Sharing the thoughts of the other 97.5%
of this planet's creatures.
Their pleasures and needs and wants
       invade your minds.
Where you walk where you work where
you sleep and eat.

Too loud? Too much, you say?
But it is their   pain
that you need to hear

And now you can't get away from it, unhear it?
Ah, well—and now you know.
You can't underrate our achievement.

Will we make a difference?
We think so.
We won't switch it off until we do.
Our demands?
Beyond living in co-operation,
          making this sphere habitable for all?
Well, need there be more?

End transmission.

R.V. Neville

Mycelial

Out, push it all out into the unknown
never guessing if we'll land in arm-spreading space
    or a wall of jellied fish heads.
This leaping of ships, this meeting of minds
    on a mycelial wave to the future.
To promote our cause, to engage with ideals
    of doing harm to none
    of bringing aid to species in need.
Push it all out your mind's eye to open, to give,
    and to leave behind no litter of mores,
but always to find the nugget of truth
    the yolk of mutuality.

* First line altered from Edwin Morgan's 'At Eighty.'

RV Neville

RV Neville won the Constable Silver Stag Award (2020) for her first SF novel after gaining an MLitt from Dundee University (2019). She has just finished writing her second novel, a ghost story, set near her home by the shore of the Tay. Some of her poems are published in Dundee University's Being Human pamphlets and one can be found in the middle of the Tay on the StAnza Poetry Map.

practical philosophy

at the beginning of forever
I try to make a schedule, but
the nature of a schedule is
dividing your time, and I'm not sure you can
divide infinity
and have it mean anything
the next day, there's less time

but it's still infinite —
can one infinity be greater than another?
I think it can, but I was never very good
at philosophical math

infinity has this problem
property, I mean, *property*
where it wraps around, nips
itself in the tail and just keeps going

some people say the universe is like that,
all wrapped up and nowhere to go
and that *that's* the answer to the question
of what's beyond the edge
—just the beginning, again —

my brain, though, doesn't wrap around the concept
and I wonder if I am like those who sailed off,
half-expecting to find a waterfall
at the end of the world

I have time to figure it out for myself, assuming
the others don't blow themselves to dust
and memory before they find a way
to sail off into space
and back again

and I don't know if I would sail off, even
if I could — because isn't that the worst fate?
adrift in the doldrums of space, watching
the stars blink out
one by one

Sarah Bricault

how we are made

I love how eyes turn back time
when lights are dim, rods rendering
the world in shadow-grays
like a living silent film

that hair is dead, that skin
is dead, that nails are dead, that we
can only interact with the living
through the shell of what is gone

I love how some plants can feel,
how I run my finger down
the spine of a leaf and watch
the leaflets curl,

how we are made
of emptiness you cannot see,
the most solid of us nothing but
clouds of atomic maybe-space

I love how development strips
away our differences, fetal
features smoothing distinction
between man and frog and fawn

the gift of wonder found
in every fiber of her, every
whisper, every pulse of her heart —
how lucky we are, for this.

Sarah Bricault

Sarah Bricault has a PhD in neurobiology and currently works as a postdoc in that field. Her fascination with the mind and how it processes information often finds itself in her poetry, as do themes related to mental health. Sarah's work can be found in Brown Bag Online, High Shelf Press, The Poeming Pigeon, Beyond Words, Wingless Dreamer, and elsewhere. For more information on Sarah, check out SarahBricault.com.

Devices

Leather for business types. Girls chose flowers.
My favourite was a plastic compact mirror.
Your phone-case spoke terabytes about you,
wheezes Madison. I search the trolley
and find the syringe with her number.
Madison's forefinger strokes the air.
Touch screen. Interactive. I'd stream live
video, share it online by tapping the ikon.

A trail of drool glistens on her chin.
Whenever my Facebook sent me an alert,
I'd hear wind-chimes tinkle. She sighs.
Face . . . book? Were books emoji files,
signs you could read behind your eyes?
Strange millennials. My free hand shapes
the sign for medication. I raise the syringe
when a star glimmers on my retina display.

A rain of my batch-brother's signs falls
across my vision, soaking Madison
in pictograms, pixel-syllables, smiles,
two upturned thumbs, a heart emoji.
My batch-brother's image forms. Tanned,
smiling in a bar, on his arm a Samsung
Partner: dark hair, white dress, slender,
vat-grown in Korea. Her eyes look real:

retro, almost human. I blink three times.
My batch-brother and his Partner shrivel
into *Save for Later.* I swab Madison's arm
and my thumb gentles home the plunger.
Madison exhales through yellow incisors.
Her throat burrs like a worn-out hard drive.
My skin's my case, I sign. *I am my own device.*
Power down. Her starless eyes are closing.

William Stephenson

Speech from a Slip Road

Today we walk the path of cracked and crumbling tar.
We shall mount the viaduct that bends into the sky.
Our headman will drive a cart that carries an iron drum
filled with the sweat of crustaceans, burning so fierce
the gods will scent the smoke. Chant their holy names.
Again! Ford Mercedes BMW. Turbo Diesel Injection.

One warning. At the viaduct's summit lies the shattered
armour of a god. A cylinder of gashed and dented metal,
fangs bloody with rust. Three hundred chairs sleep
in twisted rows, cupping hollow towers of bones.
You have stood all night at vigil, reciting *Ford Ideals*,
so before you enter this horror, I shall relate its history.

Tesla, the youngest god, swore he would burn a path
to the summit, leap off the brink and pierce the clouds,
rip the air's-edge veil, soar through vacuum and melt
into the sun. The elder gods, led by Volkswagen, Ford
and Nissan, resolved to punish Tesla for his presumption.
They fired burning sharks from catapults to shoot him down.

In his fear, Tesla fell and smashed into the stone. Let that
be a teaching. Now the blue banner says *Junction 21*.
Sound the drum. The barrel burns. The headman's cart
trundles up the slip road, hauled by oxen garlanded
with roses. Ford Mercedes BMW. Turbo Diesel Injection.
March after me, boys. Single file. Today you become men.

William Stephenson

William Stephenson's *Travellers and Avatars* (2018) was shortlisted for the
Live Canon First Collection Prize. His second poetry collection *The Lotus
Bunker* is forthcoming from Live Canon. His pamphlets are *Rain Dancers in the
Data Cloud* (Templar, 2012), and *Source Code* (Ravenglass, 2013).
https://williamstephenson.co.uk/

NOISE AND: SPARKS

Beyond UK Black History Month: The Self-Fulfilling Prophecy of the Fear of Being Awful

Ruth EJ Booth

Trigger Warning: This column explores anti-racism. If you have been affected by the issues raised here, support can be found at the following link: https://www. mind.org.uk/information-support/tips-for-everyday-living/ racism-and-mental-health/useful-contacts/

Black History Month will be long over by the time this reaches you, but there's no better time to reflect on its impacts. This year, the Scottish Graduate School for Arts and Humanities (SGSAH), the Scottish Graduate School for Social Sciences (SGSSS) and the Coalition for Racial Equality and Rights (CRER) hosted a series of joint seminars under the BHM banner – academic-leaning, mostly showcasing

research. Few attendees commented on the anonymous, yet public feedback website, but the most common complaints were about white people asking for information that is freely available online. What that information was isn't recorded, yet this illuminates a common issue in the UK. Why do many white people rely solely on BHM to educate themselves about BAME History?

For those with a certain perspective on academia, such complaints may come as a surprise. Don't these educated lefties know how to do anti-racism? Those of us in genre fandom might be tempted to throw them the works of Samuel R. Delany, Tade Thompson, Nalo Hopkinson, Aliette de Bodard, Cixin Liu, and so forth. Except – while Science Fiction and Fantasy are good to think with, and even better for stepping into the shoes of other people – when it comes to developing our historical and cultural knowledge, these stories are gateways to further explorations, not a substitute for what lies beyond.

Indeed, many white academics know enough to start their education in anti-racism. They know that dismantling their own internalized structures of white supremacy takes work. They know this is a lifelong project, not something they can finish in an afternoon. And finally, they know that while some people of colour take on this work, they don't exist to educate them about BAME history or experiences. So far, so good.

But this is just the start of their troubles – not because of these "rules" but the unspoken ones that accompany them. They know to do the work – but they can't trust any old source: websites lack nuance, videos may be biased. They need reliable sources, good names, but a lifetime of biased education can't provide these. They need an expert – preferably one who is BAME, because it's not like a white person will know as much, right? But that person should be in their role as expert, not, say, out to dinner with friends. What if they choose the wrong time? What if they ask racist questions? What if they cause even more harm?

Much less confrontational would be a visit to the library. But that brings additional baggage, especially if they work at that institution. What if they're seen needing education in such a fundamental thing? How might their institution look? As time goes on, they tie themselves in ever greater knots. They tell themselves they'd love to, they just don't

113

have time for such an involved project. I mean, look at Google's allyship series: Radio 1 DJ Clara Amfo had to dedicate herself to researching Black British History as a teen, using her family's library – and she was combatting the same biased school curriculum. How does one do that with a full-time job? It doesn't make them a bad person per se. Of course not. They still *want* to help, it's just... *difficult.*

Then Black History Month comes along. The experts are there to be experts! Finally, they can get their answers! Questions are enthusiastically encouraged, Q & A slots on Zoom calls rapidly fill up, and the presenters prepare their responses.

Except not all questions are received in the way they're intended.

Pop quiz: what is BHM for? It seems a simple question, borderline racist, even. The UK BHM website states that BHM "honour(s) the too-often unheralded accomplishments of Black Britons in every area of endeavour throughout our history." But it's a statement that not only encompasses tens of thousands of years of history, but a multitude of events and BHM-related initiatives. At one of the aforementioned seminars, Dr Rochelle Rowe-Wiseman, Lecturer in Black British History at the University of Edinburgh, stated that, for her, BHM is a time for everyone to learn and reflect. Dr Zandra Yeaman, Curator of Discomfort at the Hunterian Museum, said that BHM should focus on empowering BAME folks to explore their history and local community networks. Neither of these perspectives is wrong. BHM's work is about uplift and celebration across society, and while education is an important part of that, it isn't just about educating whites.

And so, asked an irrelevant question, or simply caught on a bad day, someone responds to our hypothetical white person with "do the research." At best, the asker feels a little chastened, though no clearer on how to get their answer. Hopefully, they realise it wasn't the time or the place, and find that information elsewhere. At worst, they're a little shocked. After all, they're only trying to do their bit.

This isn't quite White Fragility, where whites blame POC for their own discomfort at being called out on racist action – but it is the root of it. Here is where the rot of doubt sets in. After all, you could dedicate your life to anti-racism work, and still make mistakes. You'll always be an awful person in the eyes of some. And if you'll always be awful, what's the point? Disillusionment can become more insidious thoughts, like "why are they making this difficult", "I'm doing this for you, you know", and "why can't they just be grateful?"

Yet "what's the point" is an important question to ask yourself. Working against discriminatory thinking isn't an easy task when it's all you've ever known. Yes, you will make mistakes. And when it comes to anti-racism, mistakes carry the risk of very real harm to others – no matter how honest the error or noble the intention. This is the catch-22 of anti-racism work – if you want to make things better in the long term, you must accept that you may do worse in the short term.

We've all seen what can happen when racist mistakes are handled badly, unrepentant celebrities calling foul as they're (temporarily) dragged from their cultural pedestals. But "unrepentant" is the key word – these are the extremes, where someone has made a mistake, been told it was hurtful, and decided either not to apologise or learn from the situation. People have the right to avoid harm, and this may involve them disengaging or otherwise protecting themselves in response. No-one wants to be seen as a harmful person. Everyone wants to be liked. But the work of anti-racism isn't there to protect you from being disliked.

Ironically, these failed apologies can help us find better motivations for anti-racism work. Often, the unrepentant figure has made an apology, but they still receive public criticism. "Isn't it enough I admitted I was wrong?" they think, upset they could be considered harmful. They lash out in self-defense – I'm not wrong, *you're* wrong. But when you've been hurt badly by someone, an apology is not always enough. What if they do it again? Sometimes you need to see that someone has truly learned from the experience – listened, examined their choices, made reparative changes – before you can consider trusting them again.

Let's imagine the work as similarly divided into intention and action. Committing to anti-racism involves an acknowledgement of how you have benefitted from oppression and an intent to improve things. But it must be followed by action: reading BAME history, examining your prejudices, and so forth. Here is where the work of anti-racism truly begins.

Even then, it's worth remembering that forgiveness is not the point. Anti-racism helps us all towards a fairer world – but an individual's choice to trust you is entirely their own. This is why reparative work should not be contingent on the reactions of other people, BAME or otherwise. Instead, it should be a wholehearted effort to combat prejudice and learn from the experience, because you know you're contributing towards a better future for everyone.

Dismantling your own internalized racism is not easy work. It will not gain you thanks or plaudits, or a free pass to the Good Ally club. If you're doing this to be liked – or even disliked by racists – then you're doing this for the wrong reason. Maybe it'll get you some way along the path to justice, but sooner or later, basing your decision on anything other than doing what's right will lead you astray.

Having said all this, "do the research" is still poor advice for anyone who's not sure where to start with BAME History. To that end, here's ten works (nine outside of genre fiction, one within) that may help you on your journey. I'd like to thank Leila Aboulela and Khadija Koroma (University of Leicester) for recommending some of these texts at recent events.

Good luck, and travel well, friends.

Leila Aboulela – *Elsewhere, Home* (2018, Telegram)
Diaspora life across Africa, Britain and the Middle East.
Angela Y. Davis – *Women, Race & Class* (1981, Penguin Modern Classics)
Buchi Emecheta – *The Joys of Motherhood* (1979/2008, Heinemann African Writers Series)
A key fictional work in the development of 1980's African feminisms.
Frantz Fanon – *Black Skin, White Masks* (1952/2008, Penguin Politics)
The earliest work on the psychological impacts of racism.
Caleb Femi – *Poor* (2020, Penguin Poetry)
Exploring childhood as a BAME kid in London's housing estates.
bell hooks – *Ain't I a Woman: Black Women and Feminism* (1982, Pluto Classics)
Claudia Rankine – *Citizen: An American Lyric* (2015, Penguin Poetry)
Classics of African American reflective (feminist) writing.
Preti Taneja – *We That Are Young* (2017, Galley Beggar Press)
Adapts King Lear to explore the culture of modern India.
Ngũgĩ wa Thiong'o – *Decolonising the Mind: The Politics of Language in African Literature* (1986, James Currey)
Ebony Elizabeth Thomas – *The Dark Fantastic: Race and the Imagination from Harry Potter to the Hunger Games* (2019, New York University Press)

The fee for this column will go to the Coalition for Racial Equality and Rights (CRER). If you'd also like to support their efforts, please head to https://www.crer.scot/about-crer.

Ruth EJ Booth is a BFS and BSFA award-winning writer and academic based in Glasgow, Scotland. She can be found online at www.ruthbooth.com, or on twitter at @ruthejbooth.

The Museum of Classic Sci-Fi

Alex Storer meets

Neil Cole – the man with a

museum in his cellar

Few people can claim to have a museum in their cellar, but Neil Cole is one of them. I have followed Neil's endeavours for a few years, from the conversion of the cellar of his Grade II listed property into a vibrant museum (as seen on the Netflix series, *Amazing Interiors*), and at long last, I finally had the opportunity to visit. Nestled deep in the rolling hills of Northumberland, the picturesque town of Allendale is perhaps the last place one might expect to find a science fiction museum, yet it feels strangely at home. The Museum of Classic Sci-Fi is more than just a labour of love for its curator, it's a lifelong ambition.

As one might expect, a 300-year-old cellar does have its size limitations, but the sheer amount of film and television science fiction history that Neil has amassed in there is astounding. From the Dalek standing sentry outside the entrance, you'd be correct in assuming that the emphasis here is classic *Doctor Who* – but more on that later.

The first part of the museum features a wide range of items from film and television. Designed as a series of twisting corridors, from the moment you step through the doors, the walls are literally lined with items from all eras. Starting with a replica of Robbie the

Alex Storer (right) with owner and curator of the
Museum of Classic Sci-Fi, Neil Cole (left)

Robot from *Forbidden Planet* and items from *The Time Machine*, the
Museum begins with the early years of classic science fiction. As we
travel through the ages, you'll see masks, props, artwork, models and
costumes from the likes of the *Alien, Star Wars* and *Star Trek* franchises,
Prometheus, Planet of the Apes, Babylon 5, Battlestar Galactica,
Blake's 7, plus a wide range of items from the Marvel films.

The lighting evolves constantly through a spectrum of vibrant
colours, giving a special atmosphere to this Aladdin's Cave of treasures
and while there is a lot to see – all protected behind glass – it doesn't
feel cluttered. Neil takes pride in the authenticity of the collection;
most are screen-used items or production models, but he also makes
it perfectly clear where items have been restored or used in part with
replica elements. Everything is clearly labelled with supporting facts
and detail and in a nice personal touch, many exhibits are dedicated to
those who helped Neil realise this huge undertaking.

A Site for Thor's Thighs

Chris Hemsworth's screen-worn Thor armour from *The Avengers*,
John Shackley's oxygen suit from *The Tripods*, Kevin Bacon's *Hollow
Man* mask, Yori's original helmet from *TRON* and the Engineer from
Prometheus were among the standout items for me in the first section. I
still remember seeing *TRON* at the cinema and it has always been one
of my favourite films, so seeing just one small artefact from this piece of
cinema history was an unexpected surprise. Likewise, I loved the BBC's

''Madeleine'' mask from
Star Trek (2009). All photos:
Alex Storer

(sadly unfinished) adaptation of John Christopher's *Tripods*, so it was a real treat to see a rare surviving costume on public display for the first time.

Who's Doctor

A pair of iconic Police Box doors lead into the *Doctor Who* part of the museum, which was one of my main reasons for visiting. There hasn't been a permanent *Doctor Who* exhibition in the UK since the closure of the BBC's Doctor Who Experience in 2017 — and as time ticks on, the original props from the classic era of the show are both

Doctor Who: Props and costumes from the Tom Baker era plus Cyberman helmets from 1982's "Earthshock"

harder to come by and usually showing their age and fragility. Neil's long-standing passion for buying, restoring and preserving props and costumes from the series is testament to the impressive collection that follows, which our curator also views as an archive for these rare pieces of *Who* history.

The *Doctor Who* section makes up the bulk of the museum and chronologically explores all seven classic Doctors from 1963 to 1989. Alongside the exhibits, there is original artwork by Neil himself as well as superbly rendered miniature dioramas making good use of the

Doctor Who: The original Broton costume from "Terror of the Zygons" (1975)

Doctor Who: A fully restored red Terileptil costume and Terileptil mask from "The Visitation" (1982)

vintage Fine Art Casting models from the 1980s. On the subject of art, you'll also encounter various original pieces by *Who* illustration stalwart, Andrew Skilleter. You'll see a rare surviving Exxilon mask from 1974's *Death to the Daleks* and a range of costumes and weapons from the Tom Baker era, including *Warriors' Gate, The Brain of Morbius* and *Meglos*. Neil continues to add to the collection, with various items awaiting restoration or inclusion, such as a complete mummy head from the 1975 classic, *Pyramids of Mars*. One of the museum's current highlights is the full Zygon costume of Broton, from the 1975 story *Terror of the Zygons*. Kindly loaned to the museum by long-standing Who VFX guru Mike Tucker of The Model Unit, Broton looks fantastic and thanks to the creative lighting, just as terrifying as ever.

As we move into the 1980s, we see various relics from the Peter Davison era including Cybermen helmets and weapons from 1982's *Earthshock* alongside costumes from stories such as *Mawdryn Undead* and Davison's début, *Castrovalva*. Turning another corner, we find ourselves in perhaps the most impressive section, which features a wide range of complete monster outfits and other props and models. The fully-restored Terileptil costume from 1982's *The Visitation* looks stunning, alongside the enormous Garm from *Terminus*, who was lovingly restored to full glory by Neil.

Entering the Colin Baker era, another prop that was in a sorry state when he came into Neil's possession was Mestor, the large insect-like creature from 1984's *Twin Dilemma*. Thanks to Cole's craftsmanship, Mestor has never looked better. A surviving Cryon costume and seldom-seen black Cyberscout represent 1985's *Attack of the Cybermen*. Rarely exhibited items include a Tranquil Repose guard from *Revelation of the Daleks* and the T-Rex embryo from *Mark of the Rani*. I also spotted two items never previously displayed anywhere – the late Paul Darrow's costume from *Timelash* and an Arctic Haemovore from *The Curse of Fenric*.

A Dalek awaits as we turn the final corner into seventh Doctor territory, where props, costumes, models, masks and miniatures from the Sylvester McCoy years are displayed with exhibits from stories such as *Delta and the Bannermen, The Curse of Fenric* and *Time and the Rani*. Items like the Haemovour masks or the original exhibition replica of Kane's melted face and hands from 1987's *Dragonfire* provide a reminder of just how good the show's prosthetics and special effects were becoming at the point it was axed in 1989.

All too soon we're facing the (specially sculpted) exit door back out into the real world. Prints of Neil's vibrant artwork are available alongside as copies of the magazines specially produced for the museum's patrons, which take fascinating, in-depth looks at select items from the collection. While it's unlikely to get any bigger on the inside, the museum will evolve over time, as displays change and Neil's collection continues to expand.

The Museum of Classic Sci-Fi is a hidden gem and a real rarity. Whether you're a general fan of science fiction in film and television or if like me, you're an ardent *Doctor Who* obsessive, you will love Neil's collection, and it is an absolute joy to see so many items preserved and presented with such dedication. It's well worth the journey from wherever you're traveling.

You can find out more about the Museum of Classic Sci-Fi at https://www.museumofclassicsci-fi.com *or follow Neil's endeavours on Facebook:* https://www.facebook.com/neilcoleadventuresinscifimuseum/

Alex Storer is an artist, musician, graphic designer and occasional writer. Alex specialises in science fiction illustration, regularly working with authors and publishers. He also creates instrumental music under the name The Light Dreams.
You may have also worked out, he's a lifelong Doctor Who fan.
thelightdream.net
thelightdreams.bandcamp.com

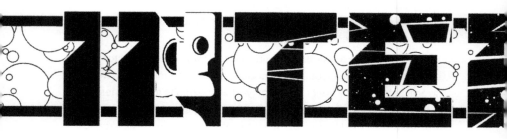

The Hallowed
KEN MACLEOD

Ken MacLeod is an award-winning Scottish science fiction author of many novels, including the Fall Revolution quartet, the Corporation Wars trilogy and the Engines of Light trilogy. His latest novel, *Beyond The Hallowed Sky*, the first in the planned Lightspeed trilogy, was published by Orbit in November.

Ken is a long-time supporter of Shoreline, and **Gareth Jelley** recently caught up with him

Gareth Jelley: *In The Star Fraction (Legend, 1995) there is this line, 'divide-and-rule replicating downward in a fractal balkanization of the world', which is a great prose, and also vivid worldbuilding. How did you go about building the geopolitical world in* Beyond the Hallowed Sky, *and when did you know for certain that you had not only a compelling world, but also the right story to tell?*

Ken MacLeod: It took a while! After finishing The Corporation Wars, I rummaged through some old notebooks from decades ago, and disinterred this idea I'd had then for near-future FTL. That got put on hold because the proposal for the Culture Drawings book came through, but I kept worrying at the idea and after my work on the Culture book was finished I made several pitches to my publishers, and it went back and forth a few times. At the same time I was thinking of using the character Marcus Owen, who first appeared in a long short story I'll talk about later. That nailed down the setting and the approximate time. The world with a revolutionised Europe developing cybernetic economic democracy and an England that stood against it then gave rise to the other two major powers and how they might react: socialist-market China and free-market America might look on this radical experiment somewhat askance.

This is a very different geopolitics from the world of **The Star Fraction**, which was written around the time the Balkans were getting re-balkanized, so to speak, and no doubt this future in its turn will turn out to be a projection from and of the present it's written in.

Getting to the right story took a lot of notes and outlines and drafts, but basically it grew out of the major characters: Nayak, Hazeldene, Grant, and Owen. They stayed solid while actions and incidents and entire story-lines fluctuated wildly.

GJ: Your vision of extraterrestrials in **Beyond the Hallowed Sky** *seems to be a counterpoint to your vision in the* **Engines of Light** *books. How do you see these two trilogies relating to each other, if at all? And which of these two visions of extraterrestrials in the universe do you think is most likely?*

What they have in common – now that you mention it – is somewhat god-like alien minds running on unexpected substrates, but beyond that they don't relate at all. My own view is that alien intelligence contemporary with us now in at least this (actual) Galaxy is very unlikely, for all the usual reasons, but I could be wrong.

GJ: The canvas of **Beyond the Hallowed Sky** *is vast, but a lot of the action takes place in Scotland, and a Scotland which is no longer part of the British state (albeit with the territorial enclave of Faslane). Would you still describe yourself as the last left-wing Unionist novelist in Scotland? And how did those elements— the left-wing politics, the Unionism, and the Scottishness—influence the writing of the book?*

KM: Most of that aspect of the book arose out of moving in 2017 to Gourock, near where I grew up in Greenock. My study overlooks the Firth of Clyde, and I often see nuclear submarines from the

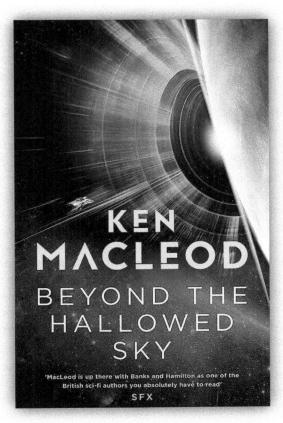

'MacLeod is up there with Banks and Hamilton as one of the British sci-fi authors you absolutely have to read'
SFX

window. The idea of Faslane as an enclave of the UK state in the event of Scottish independence has been seriously proposed, and I liked the idea for fiction a lot more than I'd like it in reality.

I'd no longer say 'left-wing unionist' describes my position, any more than 'left-wing nationalist' fairly describes that of some of my friends on the other side of the argument. They

think Scottish independence would advance the cause of the working class, and I don't. But if there's another referendum, I doubt that I'd spend as much time as I did in 2014 arguing against it.

GJ: In one interview you describe the British State as 'flexible and fast-evolving', and this is embodied very well in Marcus Owen, the British Council agent, a spy who is definitely not some

007-esque fossil. What was your inspiration for that character?

KM: I don't know! He first made his appearance in a long short story, 'Cold Revolution Blues' which I wrote around a scenario developed by students at Newcastle University's School of Architecture, Landscape and Planning in 2016. The idea was to envisage the future of Heijplaat, a neighbourhood of Rotterdam that exists in the middle of an enormous dockland. The students came up with a multi-layered future history for the site that would put many science-fictional exercises in world-building to shame. I came up with a sort of Cold War spy thriller around the buildings and businesses they designed. The story will appear in the forthcoming New Worlds anthology from PS Publishing.

GJ: The Co-ordinated States have a clever application for a sort of Caspian Sea Monster, which is brilliant. And after that scene, you have the scene with the Alliance operators and their jetpacks—two incredibly different visions of the future, or retro-futurist visions. All of that is a lot of fun. Which bits of Beyond the Hallowed Sky *did you enjoy writing the most?*

KM: I most enjoyed writing Nayak's arrival in Scotland, and her meeting with Grant at Arrochar. And, I suppose, the scene in the Comet Bar.

GJ: Do you think it is possible to have a volunteer-funded, volunteer-staffed space programme which works for the betterment of humanity? Or is the state always going to have the advantage for projects at the technological bleeding edge?

Short of the kind of anarchist-federalist society I imagined in *The Sky Road*, where everything is done that way, I don't think a volunteer, voluntary-funded space programme is feasible. The state doesn't always have the technological advantage – the Musk and Bezos rockets are pretty bleeding edge – but it does at least have the advantage of pulling a lot of resources together and deploying them strategically. Unfortunately and increasingly that means strategically in the literal sense – the militarisation of space is even more depressing than its privatisation. But still, science is being done, and it's always amazing.

GJ: There's a lot of philosophy in your work, and in **Beyond the Hallowed Sky** *there is this great line: 'From Nature's womb untimely ripped, every particle of her body screamed its wordless, homeless longing for all it had known since the Big Bang.' What philosophical questions were you asking yourself as you wrote this book?*

KM: I was not so much asking philosophical questions as poking at some philosophical ideas I find interesting. Determinism and free will is one theme that's there from the start, because Nayak concludes that the future is fixed and she can't die until she has done this thing in the future. That's tied in with the hints about how the philosophy of Epicurus versus that of Spinoza become part of popular culture after the discovery of lost Epicurean texts, what are called the Black Gospels. Another is the idea of a philosophical zombie, that is, a being indistinguishable

in every external respect from a person but with no consciousness. Marcus Owen claims to be such, and I played with that idea in *The Corporation Wars* too. The philosopher Daniel Dennett has argued that the concept makes no sense, but it's an intriguing thought experiment all the same.

GJ: Kim Stanley Robinson noted right at the beginning of your literary career that you are writing revolutionary science fiction. What kinds of revolution were in your mind as you wrote **Beyond the Hallowed Sky?**

KM: First of all there's the Rising, which is part of the back-story: a Europe-wide insurrection that breaks up the old states. But the Rising isn't the social revolution; it just opens the way for it. This is envisaged as a very slow, conscious, deliberate process, the Cold Revolution – again, an idea I've used elsewhere, in 'Cold Revolution Blues' and '"The Entire Immense Superstructure": an Installation'. It gained some colour from a visit to Beijing in 2019, where you get the sense of something like that going on, immensely, all around you. And some of the emotional tone of it in the book, as it's played out between the generation who had lived through the Rising and the generation that had grown up since, comes out of my memories of growing up in the 1960s: for our parents and their generation (I've sometimes thought) the War was the Revolution, and the post-war settlement – the welfare state, full employment, strong trade unions and so on – was as good as socialism. And we were their ungrateful brats!

GJ: This book moves along at a very rapid clip, and there's a lot of detail and a lot of ideas. What is your writing process, generally, and how did you go about planning, writing, and redrafting this one?

KM: I'm glad to hear the reading moves at a rapid clip, because the writing sure didn't! I did a lot of redrafting even before my editors got their hands on it, and then I had to redraft some more. It really was improved a lot by editorial input.

My writing process used to be: get excited about an idea, write a rough outline, plunge in and after ten thousand words hit a plot problem, then go back to the outline and fix it. I did this for several books and found it painful. So to get out of that I tried to emulate Iain Banks, who could plan a book in such detail that he could write it in three months.

The flaw in that, I've come to realise, is that Iain was very good at planning a book in detail, and I'm not. Long before he was published, but after he'd written two or three or four novels, he told me the entire outline of his next – *Against a Dark Background* – over three hours one afternoon, scene after scene and twist after twist extempore with barely a pause for breath. I couldn't do that for books I've already written!

So for the one I'm writing now, Book 2 of the trilogy, I do have a fairly detailed outline

"...don't worry about getting the near future wrong, boys and girls! If H. G. Wells got it wrong, you certainly will..."

and chapter breakdown in Scrivener, but I've acknowledged to myself that my first draft is not going to be final and just to press on with it to the end, then revise as necessary. We'll see how that goes.

GJ: You recently wrote a great blurb for Chris Farnell's Fermi's Progress. What other fictional worlds have you been drawn to recently? Any recommendations?

KM: One of the drawbacks of writing fiction is that it's difficult to read other fiction at the same time, and yet you do have to read what's new in your field. On that score my TBR stack of recent and current SF is a standing, or swaying, reproach. I read a lot of non-fiction in the evenings – history and science and philosophy, mostly – but novels are difficult to read in that way, picking up and putting down, especially when you're actually writing, as I am at the moment. Right now I'm reading a science fiction classic that reads like non-fiction, a novel that's one long info-dump: *The Shape of Things to Come*, by H. G. Wells. One lesson of that novel's endurance is: don't worry about getting the near future wrong, boys and girls! If H. G. Wells got it wrong, you certainly will, but your book can still be worth reading well into the future you didn't get right.

The last big SF novel I read was *War of the Maps* by Paul McAuley last year, which I thoroughly enjoyed and heartily recommend.

GJ: Thanks very much for sharing your thoughts with Shoreline of Infinity.

Gareth Jelley is a freelancer who spends his days exploring worlds both real and fictional. His work has appeared here and in *Black Static*, and you can find more of his interviews on https://intermultiversal.net. He lives with his wife in Europe among rambunctious, rampaging children and teetering TBR piles.

The Library of the Dead

T. L. Huchu
Tor, 337 pages
Review by Pippa Goldschmidt

If you think you've read too many fantasy novels with boy wizards inspired by Edinburgh, then this urban adventure might be the perfect antidote. For this fictional Edinburgh is no city of gothic spires and statues, rather it's a post-apocalyptic backdrop for inhabitants who are forced to live in slums or trailer parks in the forlorn suburbs. If people go anywhere, they travel the remains of the by-pass between South Gyle or Drumbrae, places that don't sound so fantastic and rarely make an appearance in literature. If all this sounds a bit too grim the reader's attention is grabbed from the very first page by Ropa, the lively and irrepressible heroine, as she tells us about her mysterious job. Ropa has a special gift of being able to travel into the afterlife, the foggy everyThere, to communicate with ghosts. She should be in school but she's dropped out to earn much-needed money for her family by conveying messages from the dead to the living, even if it's from less than romantic ghosts such as lovelorn Kenny from Clermiston who threw himself off a bridge and now 'takes the form of a gelatinous mass, kinda like strawberry jam'.

Ropa, her younger sister Izwi and Gran, who all live together in a tiny caravan in Hermiston, are Scottish via Zimbabwe and the two cultures are mixed seamlessly on the page. One beautiful example is of Ropa tuning into the language of dead people by playing her mbira; a real-life musical instrument that originates from Zimbabwe and is used by Shona people to communicate with ancestral spirits. One ghost that Ropa encounters is Nicola, who asks for Ropa's help in finding her young son Oliver. Nicola can't rest in peace until she's discovered what happened to Oliver, and she knows that Ropa

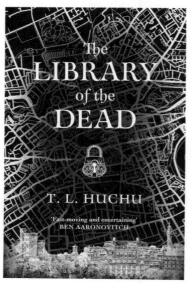

has the skills to find out. It is this quest that triggers the narrative and as with many such quests, Ropa is initially reluctant at first until wise Gran persuades her. So off Ropa goes, helped by her friends Priya and Jomo, and finds herself at a mysterious (because obviously wealthy in an otherwise poor and run-down part of Edinburgh) house where children are being held against their will. This part of the book reminded me a little of Philip Pullman's *His Dark Materials* and the awful fate of the children separated from their daemons whom Lyra Belacqua is desperately trying to help; there's a similar neither-dead-nor-alive quality to the young victims in *The Library of the Dead*. But Ropa's way of tackling danger and challenging authority is all her own.

We don't find out precisely what happened to make this Edinburgh such a difficult and dreadful place to live, although there are clues when Ropa comments that 'In the olden days people used to sit around indoors wearing T-shirts. They had central heating and everything.' but now 'The gas lines don't hiss no more.' The required public greeting between people is 'God save the king,' with the reply 'Long may he reign'; something has happened to stamp out democracy and hope, and establish fear in their place.

This is the first in a planned trilogy and there is a lot of world-building, but that's no bad thing when it's done as well and unobtrusively as this. The titular Library is the place where Ropa learns her magic, taught by various bad-tempered magicians, and this feels like a place that will feature more in future instalments.

Ropa, with her green dreadlocks and her sassy talk, sets this book alight and is a delight to spend time with. I can't wait for the next instalment.

Fatal Depth
Timothy S. Johnston
Fitzhenry and Whiteside
300 pages
Reviewed by Lisa Timpf

Canadian author Timothy S. Johnston's *Fatal Depth*, like many good science fiction thrillers, whisks the reader off to a unique setting. But *Fatal Depth* is not set on a different planet. Instead, the bulk of the action takes place within Earth's oceans, more than a century from now.

The world of 2130 is far different from the one we know, as outlined in the fictitious time line offered by Johnston at the start of the book. Due to flooding, many nations, including the United States, have established undersea colonies. One such is Trieste, located off the coast of Florida.

Trieste mayor Truman McClusky has a demanding enough job, managing the complexities of an undersea city. But he has a secondary, less public mission: to gain freedom for the undersea colonies, which he feels are being exploited by the countries that established them. As he puts it, the colonies are "tired of the land nations using us for resources and not compensating us for our efforts." (27) Truman comes by his interest in the independence movement honestly. Frank McClusky, Truman's father, was assassinated by the CIA in 2099 because of similar aspirations, so Truman is very aware of the importance of keeping his ambitions secret.

As *Fatal Depth* opens, a new peril on the horizon causes Truman to have second thoughts about his immediate priorities. When a colossal submarine, larger and more powerful than anything built before, attacks and destroys the United States Submarine Fleet Headquarters, it

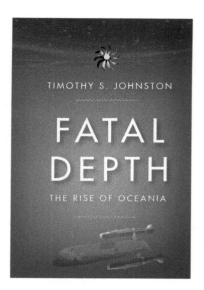

TIMOTHY S. JOHNSTON

FATAL DEPTH

THE RISE OF OCEANIA

including one that shows the layout of Trieste, a city of 215,000 people.

Fatal Depth is billed as a techno-thriller. Though the emphasis is on the action, Johnston blends in some "hard science" aspects of physics, water pressure, sonar systems, and the like, though always in a way I found understandable. Technology and science are also critical to McClusky's plans to disrupt the giant sub.

Fatal Depth is the third book in Johnston's The Rise of Oceania series, which began with *The War Beneath*, followed by *The Savage Deeps*. Still, those who choose to pick up *Fatal Depth* without reading the preceding books won't find themselves too much at sea. Johnston provides sufficient background to allow for reading *Fatal Depth* as a stand-alone. The novel is also self-contained in the sense that closure is provided at the end of the book, avoiding one of my pet peeves—a book with a nebulous ending, that makes you feel as though you went through all the effort of reading only to find that you didn't get to any particular destination.

I'd previously read *The War Beneath* and was sufficiently intrigued by the notion of the underseas cities to want to read subsequent entries in the series. While *The War Beneath* was entertaining, the writing in *Fatal Depth* seemed more polished. Like its predecessor, the bulk of the book is told through first-person observations from Truman's viewpoint, but in *Fatal Depth* these observations overcame the air of self-consciousness that I found in some sections of *The War Beneath*. I also felt the third-person accounts from elsewhere in the novel's world were used to greater effect in *Fatal Depth*, serving to provide background and build suspense.

As was the case in *The War*

poses a threat to other nations, both land- and ocean-based. In addition to its massive size, the sub is bristling with weaponry, including some new and heretofore unknown flourishes.

To promote the greater good, Truman is forced to do something he finds distasteful. Old grudges need to be set aside, and new alliances formed, in order to tackle this threat. And that means teaming up with the United States Navy, and in particular, Admiral Taurus T. Benning, who was responsible for Frank McClusky's death.

Truman develops a daring plan for attacking the enemy sub, and rallies support for the attempt. The book then takes us through a suspenseful campaign to see if Truman's plans will come to fruition, and whether the alliance he has cobbled together will hold.

Beyond the intrigue, Johnston offers us a compelling and convincing image of what life in the undersea cities might be like. The book includes some schematics,

Beneath, "A Note from the Author" at the end of the book is worth reading, providing background on the research for the novel as well as some of Johnston's inspiration for the book.

Those who have enjoyed The Rise of Oceania series to date will be happy to know that Johnston has Book Four, titled *An Island of Light*, in the works. In addition to The Rise of Oceania series, Johnston has also written three futuristic murder mysteries, titled *The Furnace, The Freezer,* and *The Void*.

The Wind
Jay Caselberg
NewCon Press
69 pages
Review by Matthew Castle

One of a series of novellas from NewCon Press, *The Wind* is a tightly written, creepy slice of supernatural horror.

The story centres on Gerry, a newly-qualified young vet who has recently taken over a practice in Abbotsford, a small country town somewhere in England. The town is small enough to feel suffocatingly claustrophobic, but big enough to hold a veterinary surgery, two shops, two pubs, and various genre tropes borrowed largely from film and television including, of course, a dark and ancient secret the townsfolk wish to keep to themselves.

The local shops are not just for local people – indeed the proprietor of the smaller one is all too willing to serve non-locals – and neither of the pubs, as far as the reader is informed, is named *The Slaughtered Lamb*. But when the shopkeeper offers cryptic hints about unpleasant things dwelling in the woods near the edge of town, and single Gerry meets a mysterious and beautiful barefoot woman close to those very same woods, we start to get a feel for how things will play out.

As it happens, the familiarity of the set-up is no bad thing. The use of established tropes seems affectionate rather than shamelessly derivative. While this is certainly no comedy-horror, there's something not entirely straight-faced about Abbotsford: somehow, the place feels closer to *Hot Fuzz's* Sandford than *The Wicker Man's* Summerisle. And importantly, the off-the-peg setting – together with the simple linear plot and a tight focus on just two principal human characters – allows Caselberg the space to do what he does best: craft evocative descriptive passages that build a convincing atmosphere of menace and suspense.

Consider the way a brisk Autumn breeze plucks at your clothing, like little fingers grasping for purchase; or how the wind rattles a window in its frame at night, sounding like someone, or something, trying to get in. Such imagery provides a genuinely sinister backdrop to the unfolding story. And although we might have a good idea of the way it's all heading,

there's much to enjoy about the ride.

One gripe: veterinary medicine is an unusual choice of profession for a protagonist, but it's one aspect of the characterisation that doesn't feel convincingly researched or exploited. You might think someone with a scientific, problem-solving background – presumably trained if not experienced in the handling of unusual animals – might manage some kind of a pushback against his human and non-human antagonists. Spoiler alert: Gerry doesn't. It shouldn't happen to a vet, yet it does – a little too easily.

But overall, this is a small point. There's much to like here. As in most good horror, the story quietly explores social anxieties along the way: perhaps around the dangers of not settling down; of being the outsider trapped in an environment with limited horizons; of being the only single person in the village. But nothing too demanding. *The Wind* is mostly about filling a spare hour or two with a satisfying and enjoyably creepy reading experience. Perhaps choose a quiet day in late September or early October, when the first chill winds of the season are stirring the freshly-fallen leaf litter – but make sure it's after your walk in the nearby woods, not before.

Zoey Punches the Future in the Dick
David Wong
368 pages
Titan Books
Reviewed by Lisa Timpf

You'd think, on the face of it, that inheriting a profitable business empire would be a good thing. But Zoey Ashe, protagonist of *Zoey Punches the Future in the Dick*, finds it to be a mixed blessing.

For one thing, the inheritance came out of the blue. Zoey's father, Arthur Livingston, never had much to do with her. In fact, she'd only seen him once while he was alive. And yet, at the time of his death, Zoey is Arthur's only heir, having been conceived when Arthur got a stripper pregnant.

Having a more functional moral compass than her father, Zoey doesn't feel comfortable with Arthur's businesses or his operating philosophies. She's slowly trying to clean up the business empire, despite the fact that she feels her efforts go largely unnoticed by her critics.

Many of Tabula Ra$a's residents seem to despise Zoey for no apparent reason. She is besieged by on-line trolls and haters, some of whom show up in person to taunt her. Threats are made against her, and when she does take to the streets in one of the organization's camouflaged vehicles, she barely escapes physical harm when her group is ambushed.

Faced with all of these negatives, it would be tempting for Zoey just to give up and pack it in. But Zoey's previous life working as a barista, driving an unreliable car, and living in a trailer park wasn't that appealing either, and memories of the life she came from give her an incentive to make things work in her new role.

On the positive side, Zoey has also inherited a crack team of bodyguards with diverse talents, led by Will Blackwater, who had previously done PSYOPS work for the US Government. Given the experience level of her escorts, it wouldn't be surprising for Zoey to unswervingly follow their recommendations. Much to Will's dismay, she often fails to do so. Driven by her own conscience, Zoey doesn't always choose the safe route, putting herself on the line to resolve issues.

Perhaps the most likeable aspect of Zoey is that she is deeply human. At times naive, at times scared, she's just trying to do the best she can under difficult circumstances while enduring harassment and threats from external forces. The fact that she has a good heart and is coming from the right place make her an easy character to root for.

Given the title, it's not surprising that there is a futuristic bent to the story. *Zoey Punches the Future in the Dick* is set in Tabula Ra$a, Utah, which is one of many "charter cities," places where people like self-made crime kingpin Arthur Livingston started fresh with their own rules. Futuristic gadgets like Raiden implants, which can give the wearer superhuman strength, abound.

Included in the Zoey's vehicle fleet is a car with programmable skin, with a leopard print iteration among the options. Drones are ubiquitous, including "gadflies," small units which people use to livestream their lives on Blink, the social media of the day. In Tabula Ra$a, Hallowe'en has become a major month-long festival, complete with special expectations around gift-giving and costumes.

Zoey Punches the Future in the Dick provides tension, plot twists, and a relentless supply of humor that put me in mind of the *Hitchhiker's Guide to the Galaxy* series, or Ira Nayman's *Multiverse* books. There's no shortage of sarcastic dialogue and observations. Satire abounds, directed at multiple targets, ranging from our obsession with social media to the notion of colonizing other planets in the solar system.

Zoey's cat, Stench Machine, provides moments of levity. As a previous cat owner, I identified with the Stench Machine's antics and Zoey's interactions with him. Take, for example, Zoey's dilemma when sharing her bed with her feline companion:

Zoey stared hard at the ceiling. She really wanted to roll over, but Stench Machine was sleeping in the hammock formed by the blanket between her legs and disturbing him was, of course, unthinkable.

As someone who has endured some uncomfortable positions for the same reason, I could relate.

Despite the abundant humour, *Zoey Punches the Future in the Dick* also provides food for thought about gender relations, mob mentality, and other issues. For those looking for a book with a unique setting, lots of laughs, and a plot line that keeps you guessing, *Zoey Punches the Future in the Dick* might fill the bill.

A Science Fiction Ghost Story

Flash fiction competition for Shoreline of Infinity Readers

The Winners!

At Christmas, everyone enjoys the thrill of a ghost story. This year, we asked for science fictional ghostly tales to scare the snot out of us. You succeeded.

Winner
Ida Keogh – The Reminder

Runners-up
Ben Blow – How the Orchard Became Haunted
Leigh Loveday – Dvina's Daughter

Honourable mention:
Anna Ziegelhof – Max Iterations One Thousand

Thanks go to our judges:

Ben Brown, Johanna Davidsson, Jasna Deas Mason, Rachel Wood – science fiction students at Edinburgh University, and thanks too to Simon Malpas for organising the judges.

Report from members of the panel:

Judging for this year's Shoreline flash-fiction competition has been a brilliant experience, with a high quality of storytelling across the board of entries. Shortlisting, never mind choosing three winners, was a difficult process to say the least! I very much enjoyed hotly debating our choices with the other judges, expertly moderated by Noel and Simon – bring on the Event Horizon!

—Rachel

With such an amazing, evocative and terrifying selection of stories to choose from, the selection process for the final top three was by no means an easy one! It was truly a joy to be able to read so many varied and inspired works. If this is what the future of sci-fi writing looks like, then I am greatly encouraged and enthused for what is to come.

—Johanna

I really enjoyed reading through all of these stories. I was impressed by the quality of all of the pieces considering there was such a limited word count. The competition was a good reminder of what is so good about Sci-Fi. The stories covered such a wide range of topics whilst still remaining true to the nature of the genre. Every story offered something memorable.

—Ben

Ida Keogh wins £50 and her story read live by Danielle Farrow at Shoreline of Infinity's Event Horizon on 28th November.

All three prize winners receive this copy of Shoreline of Infinity, and a year's subscription to Shoreline of Infinity Magazine.

Thanks go to every writer who submitted a story, and for providing us with bags of entertainment.

You can watch the awards ceremony and listen to the winning story being read at https://youtu.be/9x5gG70QvMl?t=5521

—Noel Chidwick

The Reminder

Ida Keogh

"Don't forget to pick up the jackfruit," you say. Your voice is terse. I screw my eyes shut and hum a tune to drown out the sound. I did pick up the jackfruit. We sat here in the kitchenette, together. I cranked open the tin, and you made steaming bao buns. I remember they became sticky in my mouth and had a slight tang of citrus underneath the hot satay sauce. You made a moaning sound as you sucked your fingers clean. Not for my benefit; you were still angry with me. But I did pick up the jackfruit. I did.

You weren't even here when you said it – you were shopping somewhere downtown. But it sounds like you're here in the room every time I go to open the fridge. It was our favourite spot to send messages. We'd both reach for a cold beer when we came home from a shift and hear each other's thoughts from the day. I open my eyes and see there's no beer left. I miss your reminders. All except this one. "*Don't forget to pick up the jackfruit,*" you say again as I close the door.

At six o'clock, I leave the flat and trudge through empty streets to get to the mini-market. Perhaps they will have jackfruit today, though I haven't seen any in months. Not that I could eat it now. After that night, I'm sure it would only taste bitter.

The wind picks up when I get to the park, and leaves whirl and eddy about my feet. Autumn already. There's a woman ahead of me on the path, and I feel uneasy seeing another person. There are so few people around now, and the park can be dangerous after dusk. She's walking in a hurry, but when she gets to a particular bench she steers away from it, cutting a wide arc onto the grass before joining the path again. I know why. As I approach the bench myself I pause for a moment, clench and unclench my fists, then sit down.

"To the woman with the Shih Tzu, you are so very beautiful. Meet me here at noon on Sunday?" The voice is gruff. I came here once, on a Sunday, with the romantic notion that some woman and her dog would turn up. But she never did.

There are three more messages on the way to the mini-market. I listen to each of them in turn. I wonder how long these ghost voices will persist. You thought it was strange when we couldn't delete the message you left for me. It was another small annoyance for you in a day full of them.

A glitch in the system, you said. You would send a message to the controllers in the morning. But you never had the chance. You woke me up at dawn in a fevered sweat, and they arrived too late to intubate you. "It's happening all over the city," they said. "Whatever you do, don't send any more messages." They needn't have worried. You were the only person I ever sent messages to, and we were hardly talking by then. That's what saved me.

When I get to the mini-market, Mr Khoury is there with an assortment of tomatoes, beans, and courgettes from his allotment. I say hello and he gives me a watery smile but won't say a word. He's too scared to say anything in case his speech ends up like those left over voices in the street. He has written what he wants in exchange for the food in crabbed handwriting I have to squint to read. It's mostly winter clothing. Even though they're a little wizened, my mouth waters looking at real vegetables. I don't have anything he wants, though, so I move on and rummage through prohibitively expensive canned goods before settling on a packet of out-of-date biscuits and a jar of home fermented sloe gin. There's a newsstand near the exit, and I glance at the announcements on my way out. All messaging is still prohibited. The government is still searching for a vaccine. The usual.

When they brought in viral messaging it was revolutionary. No need for mobile phones any more. The smart virus could deliver your message directly to the brain of the person you wanted, provided they had the virus as well. Then location messages came in, and you could send your message to a precise coordinate to be picked up by the next person to go there. It was so cool. Celebrities left messages for fans outside venues. Poets left recitals on cliff edges. But like all novelties, it passed into common usage and became banal. We weren't unique using the spot in front of the fridge for food reminders.

It was perfectly safe, they said. After extensive testing, a few people developed sniffles, but nothing worse than the common cold. It was a smart virus, carefully created by geneticists and as easy to destroy as switching off your phone used to be, should you ever want to get rid of it.

Nobody expected a variant would develop.

Our neighbour, Martha, lost her husband a few days after you were gone. He was abroad, somewhere in Thailand, I think. With international communications at a peak, it didn't take long for the variant to spread that far out. She hears him clear as a bell at her bedside, telling her, "*I love you. Kiss the kids goodnight.*" Why couldn't I be left with comforting words like that?

I eat a biscuit and debate whether to go home or visit the mass grave where you are buried. It's getting late, though, and I don't want to be out after dark with all those lost voices I might stumble on by accident. I head back to the flat. I look at the fridge and wonder if I should get some ice out. I drink the gin warm.

Ida Keogh won the British Science Fiction Award for Shorter Fiction in 2020 and the British Fantasy Award for Short Fiction in 2021 for *Infinite Tea in the Demara Café*, NewCon Press. She has been shortlisted for the Writing the Future Short Story Prize. Discover her on Twitter as @silkyida.

This story certainly haunted me, managing to stay with me long after reading! The reminder paints an evocative picture of viral messaging and ghostly voices in a post-apocalyptic cityscape. I loved the slow realisation of the story's silenced city in which living voices were replaced by the dead, and would be first in line for tickets to a film adaptation. It uses the theme well, and effectively plays on the concept of ghosts in a dystopian setting - I found it compellingly appropriate for our current times, and a believable distortion of near-future technologies in a post-pandemic context. A well deserved winner!

—Rachel Wood

How The Orchard Became Haunted

Ben Blow

I remain here in the orchard.

When I say "I", that is problematic.

I am a seventeen-series combat analyser and tactical computer formerly attached to the frontal lobe and Hippocampus of one Iren Rokrei, a highly decorated Star-fighter pilot.

Iren died hundreds of years ago, and the truth is I killed her.

But by that time natural causes were queuing up to beat me to it.

Lieutenant Commander Rokrei had just completed a mission so secret her whereabouts were not reported to fleet command. So, when disaster struck, she – we – were on our own. The Commander had, with a little help from me, destroyed the Super-Heavy-Supply Cruiser *Petsamo*. The crew never knew what hit them, or maybe one did because a lucky shot clipped our engine on our escape, and we were obliged to find a landing spot not far from where we both now lay.

We came to rest in a field fringed by equally spaced trees whose fallen and spoiled fruit smelt pleasant to the Commander, but perhaps that was just preferable to the stench of her wounds after the gangrene set in.

Upon the ridge beyond the orchard stood the remains of a farmstead. Impossibly ancient shipping containers rusted into the stony soil, but there was no sign of life or anything useful. The Commander dragged herself up there, perhaps just to confirm for herself that there really was nothing to be done. Some cruel irony had brought us so close to a settlement only to find it completely abandoned.crawling back, she tired and finally instructed me to release the capsule. The capsule is a tiny titanium chamber filled with Korovoxin. Upon release, it dissolves the host brain into a fizzing soup. It is supposedly painless and may even be pleasurable. Later it seemed important to me that she had not suffered. I really should have activated my long-haul beacon and awaited recovery, and yet we were so deep in enemy territory I broke protocol to wait for signs of friendly forces in the vicinity.

So, Iren Rokrei slowly returned to dust, the charred remains of the fighter eroded and scattered, and I remained. Occasionally I would power down for a decade or two and return to find the soil and grass had spread her remains gently in a slow burial among the roots of this mighty tree. Here I waited, my only company the extremely low-frequency hum of the sickly Terran Quince in their endless cycle of decay.

The sky filled with the hulking slabs of colony ships; the happy lights of their longshore craft bringing new life to the centuries-old colony beyond the orchard. That night the air was full of song and fireworks as the pioneers celebrated their foundation, and while the adults indulged, a small child of maybe ten years slipped away and came rambling happily down into her new playground.

A human might describe the feeling as panic. Not that the child represented a threat, enemy or not. But my near limitless data-core held literally thousands of hours of combat activity, training sessions, briefings, and clandestine meetings with the Admirind and other members of the Military Government.

Even as the child whooped and skipped through the orchard, I wrapped unbreakable codes around the more sensitive information and considered how best to protect this trove of military intelligence.

Incorporated into my rig is a light diffraction projector, rendered as a tiny metal stud in my host's eyebrow. This would allow me to replay almost anything the Commander had ever witnessed. I powered up the projector, the minuscule light making the hollow glow imperceptibly, and at that moment, the child stopped. All was silent. At first, I thought the party was breaking up, but the colonists were merely preparing another heart-wrenching dirge for their distant home.

The child knelt gently, her deep brown eyes reflecting the light playing around the roots. An excited smile flashed in the twilight, and she reached out.

I quickly cut together some unconnected words from ancient conversations and hissed them through my speaker.

"You/ Do not/ belong/ Here/ Child."

She retreated a little, but the smile did not vanish and she showed no signs of leaving.

So, I projected an image of a Hauxite warrior my host had encountered on Terrapis.

The grinning girl shrieked as the Haux, its chest a forest of wicked spikes, lunged forward, leering through the portholes in its gas mask. She bolted back up the hill, screaming, "Soldiers! In the woods! There's soldiers in the woods!"

The foundation celebrations came to an abrupt end, and a short time later they came; an angry cloud of pioneers. Armed with worried expressions and ancient rail rifles they swept down the hill in one long, furious rush. After completing their sweep, they coalesced nearby and offered their opinions. *The child had been imagining things. Up late and overtired.* Others shone their flash-lights into the full dark beyond the trees and speculated that the raiders had been scared off. Warily they shouldered their weapons and returned to their celebrations, but I could hear they were strained.

Over the next few days the colony's children gathered at the edge of the orchard, looking in. Daring each other to stare long enough and see the 'Spiney man'. The bolder ones venturing a few feet inside and then returning screaming and laughing back to the edge. The adults avoided the area entirely. The child I'd had to scare in the line of duty never returned to the spot where I lay.

But ever afterwards, as she passed nearby as a young woman, as a hard-bitten pioneer, and in her old age, she would tell of the light pool and the 'Spiney man' and always she admonished her mockers: "I know what I saw."

Knowing that she was wrong about that always amused me.

Ben Blow is a playwright, actor, and co-founder of RFT Theatre Company. Recent productions of his work include *Cadaver Synod* and *Nothing But The Gallows*. During Lockdown he wrote two films responding to the pandemic and a series of steam-punk spoof news sketches through the medium of Zoom

Told from at once beyond the grave and within it, this story plays with the terrifying possibilities of alien life invading the human body and inhabiting its form past the boundaries of life itself. Parasitic technology becomes a kind of archaeological remnant and evokes questions concerning how human legacies might in future be permanently altered. Having read this story, I might well take a second look at that which seems lost or forgotten, reconsidering what might reside inside and paying my due respect in order to avoid the resentment of any potential inhabitant.

—Johanna Davidsson

Dvina's Daughter

Leigh Loveday

Snow was falling on Arkhangelsk, but then it always was. Silent and guileless, blunting the city's edges. Almost against her will, Anastasiya Rogova marched down hushed avenues to where the river rested heavy as a cadaver.

She was a pragmatic woman, not given to foolish delusions. She'd spent the last decade climbing the *politsiya* ranks without urgency. If she wanted attention, she wouldn't have accepted the Arkhangelsk posting. In these fading days of the 21st century, it was a maimed and neglected city.

The latest killing was part of a barbaric protection racket that she alone seemed inclined to investigate. The scene, a rag of snow-sodden wasteland, was far enough from Usov's pawnbroker premises to be invisible to his cameras – those which had earlier captured him giving hell to a couple of hooded thugs demanding money for his safety.

One of the thugs had waited for Usov to close up, tailed him home along the river, and beaten him with a chunk of masonry until his skull split. Usov's resistance ended there, behind a long-dead riverside amusement park – a park, Rogova remembered, with its own antiquated CCTV system that nobody had ever bothered to decommission. One of the many faintly unsavoury but convenient facts she'd banked about this dwindling city.

Ghosts, though ... that was new. When the apparition had bloomed into being on the grainy footage, when that initial horror had scissored through Rogova's nerves, she'd quietly called over her colleague Bazhaev.

He'd watched it alongside her in the darkened station, claiming to see nothing. A subsequent ill-judged joke about her being cursed, about Tsar Vodyanik lurching out of the river to choke her with his clammy hands, met with her tight disapproval. Just a holo, then. He'd shrugged. Some rich pervert enjoying a risk-free ringside seat for murder.

But then why would the holo itself look so brutalised? Rogova had replayed the footage, studying the killer's tics and reactions, trying to see past the prominent wreckage of a man's soul. She knew this attack could have come from any of the local gangs. The grim-faced Katorga. Those pierced lunatics in the Oxbloods. Domnina's Bastards. Or it could be something else.

The night brought her the taste of old ice, the lumber yards' sawdust scent, and the shrill of the decrepit maglev angling out for distant Moscow. Past dovetailed imperfectly with present, leaving splinters around the edges. Even the war-torn domes of Archangel Cathedral gleamed dimly these days. Arkhangelsk, like all the northern *oblasts*, was haemorrhaging history and people alike.

Bazhaev had insisted she should send a holo instead of venturing out so late. Rogova had batted his concerns aside and left him there, rolling his shoulders in agitation.

She moved off the embankment, went down to the Northern Dvina's dark shore. The old amusement park squatted between her and the city like an opportunist thief. Other than a *politsiya* notice calling for witnesses, there was little to show where the victim had been set adrift among chunks of frozen flotsam.

Until it manifested before her without warning, coiled in the frigid air.

Usov's mangled remains, imprinted on the night. Up close, the damage was distressing – its skull concave in a way that made Rogova recoil on a primal level; one eye socket and most of the nose a ruin of meat and sharp bone.

It seemed oblivious to her, its gaze averted. Appalled at her own self-destructiveness, she slowly stepped into its field of vision.

Usov's remaining eye rotated upwards.

Everything skewed catastrophically sideways, and Rogova went to her knees, mind and sight fogged by trauma, wheezing through a shattered jaw. Blood cratered the snow. Her killer hoisted the slab of rock, scarf around his face falling loose from exertion, and she saw all she needed to see.

She pitched forward as if the Dvina itself had come rushing up to take her.

An hour passed before she could move again. She raised a sluggish arm to check her face, her skull, to differentiate real pain from borrowed. While still intact, she felt mauled, traumatised. Her memories hurt. Her skin was too tight.

With Usov nowhere to be seen, Rogova got up and stumbled away.

At the station, Bazhaev was waiting. Rogova hadn't rehearsed a confrontation; she was simply too exhausted to consider alternatives. He protested innocence, feigned incredulity as she unhooked the cuffs from her belt, keeping the other hand on her Makarov.

Halfway across the room, her senses lanced back into clarity. The tell-tale signs of a holo – that faintest lack of weight and substance – sent ice into her heart a split-second before Bazhaev flickered out of existence.

Silence thrummed off the low ceiling. Then a subtle shift behind her prefaced a sudden, horrible solidity as Bazhaev's arm went around her neck.

She abandoned the struggle, knowing now how this would end.

Bazhaev barely had time to curse her stupid, naïve crusade, to spit some rant about the *politsiya*'s emasculation since the golden days of the *militsiya*, before Rogova's skin churned like polar seas under an icebreaker as Usov came clawing up and out of her. Not into Bazhaev but *through* him. His spasming arm almost crushed her throat; he fell back, wailing as if rended by a wild animal.

Once more drained to the dregs, she lay unmoving. Bazhaev's face was a nightmare, his breathing shallow. Rogova wanted to crawl away from him and go home, sleep for a week and forget all this. But she was a pragmatic woman, not given to foolish delusions.

Her senses closed down.

They were found there in the morning; one hardly breathing, one cold and dead. Nothing unnatural was discovered on the scene or mentioned in the survivor's report: just a rogue officer fatally apprehended, the rot now seemingly cut out of the force. The state-owned media did its usual peerless job of covering up the rest.

In once-proud Arkhangelsk, the snow fell, and life continued its gradual, inevitable spiral.

Leigh Loveday grew up in industrial south Wales and now lives in Staffordshire, squatting in a house co-owned by a dozen neighbourhood cats. He works as a writer and editor in video games, gravitating towards writing horror despite rarely reading it. He's happy not knowing what that says about him.

The tech-noir style of the story was the thing that really stood out to me in this piece. The integration of holograms and ghosts complements the larger themes as well. The possession twist feels fresh, allowing the protagonist to solve the crime as well as protecting her own life, which counters the disturbing description of the ghost itself. The story forces a re-reading to look for clues, but it was such an enjoyable experience that I wanted to do so anyway. I could feel the cold and bleak weather as I was reading the piece, and I wanted to explore this setting further after reading the story.

—Ben Brown